"Bait your hook for Prince Charming, and win big!"

Aghast, Lissa stared at the sign. Steve was actually going to have his own booth at the town festival. He was actually going to try the ugly sandal on every woman in town, hoping like mad to solve the puzzle of who had fallen through his ceiling.

His scheme was doomed to failure because she would never try on that sandal.

What if someone else had exactly the same size foot? But why did that matter to her, and why did it bother her so much that every woman who tried on the shoe also got a consolation prize of a kiss from "the true Prince Charming," as Steve was billing himself.

She tried to forget how easily he had charmed her, but failed miserably. He was a charmer, and charmers were bad news...no matter how intoxicating their kisses....

Dear Reader,

Another Valentine's Day to celebrate with two very special LOVE & LAUGHTER titles. Popular Judy Griffith Gill has written another winning romantic comedy. Our hero is so convinced he has found the right woman for him when all she leaves behind is an ugly sandal that he begins the official Cinderella search.

Stephanie Bond continues her delightful duet with *WIFE Is a 4-Letter Word*. This time the groom who was abandoned at the altar in *KIDS Is a 4-Letter Word* finds his perfect match in the woman he least expected to love!

I hope Valentine's Day brings you both love and laughter.

Malle Vallik

Malle Vallik
Associate Senior Editor

THE CINDERELLA SEARCH
Judy Griffith Gill

Harlequin Books

TORONTO • NEW YORK • LONDON
AMSTERDAM • PARIS • SYDNEY • HAMBURG
STOCKHOLM • ATHENS • TOKYO • MILAN
MADRID • WARSAW • BUDAPEST • AUCKLAND

ISBN 0-373-44038-3

THE CINDERELLA SEARCH

Copyright © 1998 by Judy Griffith Gill

A funny thing happened...

My good friends tell me I'm warped. This, to my great shame, may be true. Recently when lunching with a group of fellow writers, I thought it would be fun to place our order and then, in the server's absence, all get up and move one place to the right. It would, I argued, be a great chance for eight writers to observe the behavior of a confused waitress. My friends refused! One friend suggested the experiment might result in a bowl of soup in my lap. Perhaps she was right. But still, one day...

—Judy Griffith Gill

Books by Judy Griffith Gill

HARLEQUIN LOVE & LAUGHTER
7—THERE'S SOMETHING ABOUT THE NANNY
25—LADY ON TOP

This book is dedicated to Malle Vallik, with
thanks for her unbelievable patience.

1

"THE ATTIC? You want me to crawl around in the attic?"

Lissa Wilkins stared in disbelief at Rosa Macurdy, the Madrona Inn's breakfast cook, who stood before the front desk, rain dripping from her curly gray hair, her long, spare form stooped under the weight of a brown backpack. "There are spiders up there!"

"Hush!" Rosa glanced furtively around, though at eleven-fifteen on a Friday evening, Lissa couldn't think who might be there to overhear. The elderly guests who came year after year to the rustic inn and the peace of Madrona Cove, were long since in bed. The younger ones who came for fishing and fun were still at Chuckles, Madrona Cove's favorite watering-hole and social center.

"Don't kill the messenger," Rosa said. "I don't want you to go up there." She pulled at the straps of the backpack, trying to remove it. Lissa rushed out from behind the desk and caught the heavy weight, easing it down Rosa's back. "Reggie wants you to," Rosa added, shrugging her shoulders in obvious relief. "Reggie *needs* you to."

Reggie, the inn's handyman, was supposed to have put the tapes in the attic over Steve Jackson's bed hours ago, while Steve, the most unwanted guest the Madrona Inn's staff had ever dealt with, was at the bar across the street.

Lissa set the pack on the desk. "Why does Reggie 'need' me to do it? He's the handyman. I'm the night clerk. Somehow, I don't think attics and spiders are in my job description. Nor," she added, "is toting around heavy packs in yours. You have to be on duty in less than five hours. You should be home in bed, Rosa."

Three months short of retirement, Rosa was beginning to look her age. The job was too hard on her. Lissa wished her father would get his act together and marry Rosa.

"Reg sprained his ankle," Rosa explained. "Your dad's upstairs right now making sure the springs and wires are all fixed right."

"You let my dad go up those stairs?" Lissa all but yelled. Her father should not, in her opinion, be climbing three flights of stairs.

"Will you keep it down?" Rosa glanced around nervously again. "Besides, you know your father. How was I supposed to stop him? He was the first one Reggie phoned when he sprained his ankle. Just lucky I was with him at Chuckles when Reggie tracked him down there. I couldn't keep him out of the inn or off the third floor, but I can keep him from traipsing around in the attic."

She paused and pinned Lissa with a cast-iron stare from under her eyebrows. "With your help."

Lissa nodded. "Sure. Okay." She'd do a lot more than clamber around the attic to help her dad. Two years ago, she'd given up a job in a big city hotel to do just that, though it hadn't been such a great sacrifice. This elaborate trick they were organizing might be though, what with the spiders she knew were up there...*waiting* for her.

"I only wish you'd called me at home so I could have worn jeans and sneakers instead of this." She flicked at the fullness of her calf-length gathered cotton skirt. "And these!" She glanced down at her stylish leather clogs. Staff dress at Madrona Inn was generally casual, but Lissa felt more professional in a skirt, though she'd been glad to give up panty hose and high heels except for special occasions. Living on a boat made high heels impractical.

"Here, wear these," Rosa said, kicking off her well-worn Birkenstocks.

Lissa laughed. "They're too big. I'd be better off with bare feet."

"Suit yourself." Rosa patted her mouth with the back of her hand as she yawned. "But if you step barefoot on a spider, don't come crying to me."

Lissa shuddered and slid her feet into Rosa's sandals. She slung a strap of the pack over one shoulder and shuffled toward the stairs at the back of the office.

"After he measured out the distances, Reggie put a small steamer trunk on the rafters right over Jackson's bed," Rosa said, following her to the foot of the stairs. "He said all you have to do is aim for that, put the tapes in place, set the timers and then skedaddle. I'll wait here at the desk in case Jackson comes in. I'll stall him with stories of your dear, departed ghostly great grandmother."

Lissa glanced over her shoulder. "Make sure you do." She met her father as he descended the narrow service staircase. A tall, handsome man with close-cropped steel-gray curls and happy blue eyes, Frank Wilkins was obviously in his element, running an appreciative hand along the smooth, wooden stair rail. It was, Lissa thought, a lump forming in her throat, as if he were stroking the skin of an adored woman. He loved this inn, which had been the center of his life until two years ago.

As he whispered a few last-minute instructions to her, he looked as furtive as Rosa had. He and Rosa were clearly having a ball, enjoying the excitement of the conspiracy.

Conspiracy! Lissa continued up the stairs, thinking the plan ridiculous: trying to convince Steve Jackson the Madrona Inn had a ghost. But because she cared about her father and, on his behalf, about the inn, she'd go along with it. All they needed was a few more weeks, then the inn would be theirs.

Or so the whole community hoped.

But first, it was necessary to convince Steve Jackson the inn was not worth his father's money or effort.

If, indeed, he was the right Steve Jackson. But he was. Who else could he be? And why else would he be there?

Fact: the inn, property of the fifth uncaring, absentee owner in fifteen years, was for sale again. Fact: the town's purchasing committee, of which she was a member, had a bid in on it, contingent upon their raising the required funds before their option ran out. Fact: John Drysdale, the Realtor who held the listing, had offered what he called "a friendly warning" that "someone in the resort business" was more than a little interested and was considering making a cash offer.

At first Lissa's father thought Drysdale was merely trying to up the ante, but then along came a reservation for a full three weeks from a man named Steve Jackson. It didn't take a genius to put two and two together.

The Jackson resort chain was one of the largest and best-known this side of the Rockies and Steven M. Jackson Sr. had been buying up properties left, right and center for the past six years. He focused on old, rundown places, bought them for a song, tore them down and put in something bright, shiny, new and modern...the likes of which would never fit in Madrona Cove.

Well, fine. If Jackson Senior had sent Jackson Junior to check out the Madrona Inn, hoping his son would find fault so he could get away with a very low bid, the plan was to give him plenty of fault to find. Then if Jackson Resorts, Inc. made its bid, with any luck it would be lower than what the town committee had made.

And toward that end, Lissa would even brave spiders.

On the small landing outside the attic door, she stopped, checked the contents of the pack, and found everything she'd need.

She eased open the door. Up there under the roof, the sounds of the summer storm were intensified. The wind howled low and mournful, rain lashed against the shingles and beat at the small window in the gable end overlooking the Cove. She flicked on her flashlight, found the bare lightbulb hanging from a wire dangling from the roof, and unscrewed the bulb.

Setting it down carefully atop one of the dusty old pieces of junk her father happily referred to as her "heritage", she screwed in the plug socket she'd found in the backpack. With a long black extension cord plugged into that and paying out of the backpack slung once more on her shoulder, she tiptoed in Rosa's floppy sandals to the edge of the floored area.

Stretching out before her in the beam of the flashlight, were parallel rows of floor joists, along which she was going to have to navigate to get to the trunk. It looked as if it were a mile away, over there where the slope of the roof met the flat of the floor.

Sucking in a steadying breath, she put one foot on one joist, the other on the next one, and inched toward the trunk, trailing the cord over her shoulder, hoping it wouldn't catch on anything and tip her off balance.

As she neared the trunk, the slope of the roof forced her into an awkward crouch. Her full skirt threatened to trip her with each step. Pausing for a moment, she bunched it up under her arms, baring her legs, making her duck-walk more comfortable.

Finally reaching her destination, she set the pack on the trunk, took out the tape players, balanced them on a floor joist beside her, plugged in the timers, set their clocks, and hooked them up to the power bar, which she connected to the extension. The timers began to click slowly around, the first set to trigger a tape at one-thirty in the morning, the second at three-thirty.

Ghostly cries, sobs, laughter…would they disturb Steve Jackson's sleep? Would they scare him? And even more important, would they induce him to send home poor reports to his father, regarding the inn's viability as an investment opportunity?

She doubted it, but the rest of the committee thought it was worth a try.

Hoping the old gypsum board between the rafters would hold the weight of the equipment, she reached out to position the first tape player just as an enormous black wolf spider leapt out of the dark and landed square on the back of her hand.

With a scream, she jerked away, felt her feet slip,

and then she was falling, crashing through the ceiling right over Steve Jackson's bed.

THE OLD INN creaked and groaned as heavy winds and rain beat with relentless intensity against the leaded glass windows of his room. Steve felt as gloomy as the weather as he sat leaning against the pillows propped at the head of his brass bed. Some vacation this was turning out to be. Maybe he should have stayed at the bar and taken up the redhead singer-cum-dining room hostess on her tacit invitation, but he hadn't been in the mood. Nor was he in the mood for the lurid paperback thriller he'd been trying to get into for the past half hour. It wasn't living up to its hype, any more than the Madrona Inn was living up to its reputation.

Trouble was, he wasn't in the mood for a vacation, either. When his contract had run out and no one had offered him another one, he'd thought, what the hell, he hadn't taken time off for three years and now seemed as good a time as any. A low, howling wail quavered in the air for a long, tremulous moment, then stopped suddenly.

Have you met her yet? Have you seen the lady? You know the old inn is haunted, don't you?

Each time he'd been asked one of those questions by the staff at the inn or the friendly crowd in Chuckles, the local hangout, he said that he didn't believe in ghosts. And he didn't. Though that wind, if he let his imagination run free, did have a ghostlike wail to it.

A thud from above drew his gaze to the ceiling. "Idiot," he muttered. "You know perfectly well there's no such thing as— *Arrgh!*"

He screamed as a body crashed feetfirst through the ceiling accompanied by a shower of broken plaster. Dammit! He, the intrepid deep-sea diver, the fearless explorer of an alien environment, actually screamed and scrambled off the bed at high speed. Luckily, his own embarrassing bellow was drowned out by a loud, anguished feminine howl as the body came to an abrupt halt. Dangling from the hole in the broken plaster were a pair of decidedly shapely, feminine legs.

As he continued to stare, the legs began to flail, and a pair of slender feet clad in brown sandals kicked furiously in the air.

"Hold on!" Steve shouted, leaping back onto his bed. He managed to capture one warm-skinned, smooth-textured, delicate-boned ankle. The free foot then kicked him square in the face.

Blood gushed out of his nose, splashing across the white sheet and pillows.

"Let me go!" the voice demanded.

Steve blinked hard, his eyes flooded with stinging tears of pain. "Let you go? Are you nuts, or what?" To better control the legs, he wrapped one arm around the woman's knees, pinning her lower legs against his shoulder. "I'm trying to help you, so hold still!" He gave a tug and felt her body descend.

Instinctively, wanting to make her descent as smooth as possible, he placed the flat of his hand under her buttocks as they emerged.

"Get your hand off my butt, you lecher!"

"Jeez!" He moved his hand down to her thigh. "You think I'm enjoying this?" He stared upwards at a round, lush bottom covered in nothing but a pair of hot-pink panties with a dainty row of lace around the legs. "In case you haven't noticed," he added, "you're stuck in the middle of my ceiling, sweet-cheeks."

"'Sweet-cheeks?'" she repeated, her voice an indignant squawk. "Nobody calls anybody that any-more!"

Steve laughed. "They do if they've got the kind of view I have down here."

"Oh!" Even that sounded like cussing. "You're not even supposed to *be* there!" she said, renewing her futile struggles.

"Tell me about it." He wiped his bloody nose on the back of his hand. "But if I'd gotten the cabin I wanted, you might still be in this predicament, honey, though *I* sure as hell wouldn't. Now quit fighting me. Put your arms over your head. I'll pull you the rest of the way through."

"No way!" Her squirming renewed. "Push me up." It sounded like an order, but a second later she added a reluctant "Please?"

"Be a whole lot easier to get you down. Gravity, you know."

"If gravity was going to get me all the way down, it would have already done so when I fell," she answered with what Steve had to admit was excellent logic. Not that he was about to tell her so. She still had his bloody, aching, undoubtedly swollen—maybe even broken—nose to pay for. He tugged at her waist, bending his legs. The bedsprings squealed almost as loudly as she did.

She wriggled those delicious, silky limbs against his bare shoulder and chest. Feeling only a bit guilty, he realized he was enjoying it more with each wiggle. Hell, he liked legs. He liked women. He especially liked women with legs like this one had.

Looking up again, he saw something crawling out from under the leg of her panties. He swatted it.

"Ouch! Dammit, what was that for?"

He stared at his empty hand, then at the bug still perched on her rear. "I think I just smashed your tattoo. Sorry, I thought it was a spider."

She shuddered. "Perish the thought," she muttered.

"Spiders are a problem, huh?" He could relate to that. Personally, he hated moths, as irrational as he knew it to be.

"Spiders are *the* problem."

"Then let's get you out of there." As he planted his feet wide apart to steady his stance, he felt her lift away from him as if someone up in the attic was pulling her. Someone was. *She* was.

"Come on, honey," he said. "Help me here, so I can help *you.* Make like an eel and let yourself slither."

"I'm not an eel, I don't slither, and I'm not your *honey* you…you…opportunist!"

That was distinctly unfair. "Well, you sure as hell aren't a salmon, which is all this opportunist came here for," he replied. "If you think catching an ungrateful—" He stopped, sucking in a couple of steadying breaths. She was stuck. She was scared and likely embarrassed. He wasn't going to get anywhere with her if both of them were mad and hyperventilating.

Maybe if he got her to relax a little, he could get her out of this mess. Compliments. Women liked compliments. "If your top half lives up to your bottom half, maybe I'll forget about fish. You might turn out to be the catch of the season."

"Oh, sure, great, and I end up stuffed and mounted above the fireplace with a plaque under my belly?"

He laughed. "Works for me. You're a good, firm specimen, anyway. Stuffed and properly mounted, you'd be in less danger of falling down."

Suddenly, the word "mounted" took on an entirely

different connotation in his mind. As if she sensed that, she renewed her struggles and let loose a further string of curses.

Tired of arguing, tired of trying to maintain his balance on the sagging mattress, he gave another tug on the woman's legs and felt her come down a further two inches.

"Stop pulling and start pushing, Mac! That top half you're so interested in is jammed up here and you're about to rip off what I'm certain you'd consider the most important parts of it."

Oh.

"All right, all right," he said. "Up you go, then. But believe me, I want an explanation—*sweet-cheeks.*" Just barely, he resisted giving them another little pat for good measure.

Bending his knees, he wrapped his hands around her ankles and put her sandaled feet on his shoulders. With one hand on her bug, and the other splayed against the sloping part of the ceiling for balance, he boosted her up through the hole.

Suddenly relieved of her weight, he staggered backwards on the too-soft mattress, fell off the bed and landed on the floor with his back against an oak highboy. His head smashed so hard into a drawer-pull that he saw stars. While recovering on the floor from his fall, he watched a trunk come hurtling onto his bed.

It had popped open, spilling out some yellowed papers and some old clothing that smelled of mothballs.

Slowly, Steve got to his feet. Cautiously, he approached the bed. When he was sure nothing else would come tumbling down upon him, he shouted, "Hey, you okay up there?"

There wasn't a sound. Even the wind and rain had died down. "Miss? Where are you?"

Still nothing. Not a hint of a sound. No sign of movement, no face appearing in the jagged hole overhead.

Well, hell! If it hadn't been for his aching nose he'd have thought he'd imagined her. Without taking his gaze off the ceiling, he backed into the adjoining bathroom. After soaking a washcloth in cold water, he cleaned the blood off his face and neck.

Before calling downstairs to the front desk—he could only hope there'd be someone on duty at this time of night—he tugged on his jeans and shook the plaster dust from his hair.

What the hell had Ken seen in this place? It had clearly gone downhill from the time his buddy had visited fifteen years before. For a nickel he'd leave. The weather had been lousy since his arrival on Wednesday, and now the place was collapsing around his ears. Wrestling a few fish into a boat simply wasn't worth it.

IN HER FEAR and fury, Lissa all but flew down the service stairs that led from the attic to the storage room at the back of the office, and burst through the door to the reception area. Rosa stood behind the counter, ostensibly keeping an eye on the front entrance to the Madrona Inn.

"Dammit, Rosa," she demanded, "I thought you were going to stall him? Tell him about my ghostly great-grandmother? Offer him a cinnamon roll or something?"

"Huh?" Rosa whirled around to gape at Lissa. *"What happened to you?"*

Lissa started brushing the plaster dust off her blouse, then smoothed down the cotton skirt that had been crumpled up under her armpits while she hung in midair. "Jackson's in his room! A wolf spider pounced on my hand and scared me half to death. Then, if that wasn't bad enough, I fell through the damn ceiling! I lost one of your sandals up there somewhere."

"I've had those sandals since 1968!" Rosa wailed. "How could you lose one?"

"How could you let Jackson slip by you?"

"He didn't! I swear he didn't come in. I never even blinked my eyes. I couldn't have missed him."

"Then who do you suppose is in his room?" Lissa asked, but Rosa only shook her head, gnawing on her lower lip, her brows drawn tight over her small nose.

"He must have come back before your dad and I got back," Rosa said defensively, "though Gertie didn't mention it."

Gertie, the afternoon shift desk clerk probably wouldn't have, Lissa knew. Gertie saw little and said less. "Did you ask her?"

"Well, no, but your dad came right over and I only stopped off at Reggie's for the stuff. When we left the bar, Ginny was singing straight to Jackson. I can't believe he'd walk out on that."

Neither could Lissa. Ginny, her best friend since they'd both been six, had an enviable way with males that she'd begun practicing in first grade and by now had perfected. Even as a child Lissa had been awed by Ginny's captivating manner, and had long ago given up trying to match it. Men followed Ginny like lovesick puppies.

"Well, obviously, he did walk out on Ginny," she said. "Or someone else is in his room."

Of course, she had slipped into the kitchen for the carafe of coffee Jock, the dinner cook—and Ginny's father—always left for her, but that had taken mere seconds! Still, she supposed that would have been long enough for Jackson to come in and go upstairs.

Oh, heavens! Had he heard her father tinkering up there? If so, had he thought anything of it? She grinned. Maybe he had. And maybe he'd thought it was a ghost. One could always hope....

"Now, who do you suppose *that* will be?" she asked rhetorically as the phone on the desk rang its two distinctive chirps, indicating a call from one of the guest rooms.

The phone chirp-chirped again. Lissa drew a deep breath, let it out slowly, then picked up the phone. "Front desk," she said smoothly. "How may I help you?"

"A woman and a trunk just fell through my ceiling," said a very irate male voice she had no difficulty recognizing.

A *trunk?* Had she knocked it through the hole in her scramble to grab the equipment and run? "I see," she said, managing to keep her astonishment out of her tone. *Make like you don't believe him,* she told herself.

"A woman and a drunk just fell through your ceiling. Are they two separate people, or one and the same?"

"Not a drunk, a trunk! Tango, Romeo, Uniform—"

"Right," she interrupted. "I get it. A trunk, not a drunk." Oh, Lordy, she *had* knocked it down! "And a woman. They, uh, fell through your ceiling?"

"Yes, dammit, and if you don't believe me, there's blood, plaster, and old clothing all over my bed as proof. I'd like the matter taken care of at once."

Blood? Had she scraped her legs when she fell? She didn't feel injured—except dignity-wise. "Yes, sir. Certainly, sir. What room did you say you were in?" *Oh, you're good, Lissa.*

"I didn't." The words were chiseled in ice. "There's no number on my door. I'm on the top floor."

"Oh yes. That would be..." She hesitated, as if she had to check the register. "Mr. Jackson?"

In as soothing a tone of voice as she could muster, she added, "I'll be right up to investigate the incident, sir."

The receiver smashed down on the other end. Steve Jackson was definitely not impressed by the Madrona Inn, which was, of course, exactly what they'd been aiming for.

She winked at Rosa, who grinned in approval, apparently forgiving the loss of the sandal. Good, that was a relief. After all, Rosa was her de facto stepmother. Her dad and Rosa's so-called clandestine affair, which they blithely and erroneously believed to be a secret in Madrona Cove, had been going on for years.

"Oooh, he's ticked off." Lissa laughed, gave Rosa a high five and kicked off the one remaining sandal. She shoved her feet into her own shoes. Wearing them, it would have been impossible to make her way safely across the rafters in the attic to reach the spot right over Steve Jackson's bed, which Reggie had marked by positioning the trunk. Hauling up her skirt, she checked herself for scratches that might have bled. Nothing. Maybe he'd exaggerated to get faster action.

"Okay, here I go," she said, satisfied she wasn't marked with any evidence. "Desk clerk, chambermaid, and general apologist for the Madrona Inn's dreadful deficiencies. Maybe Reggie's masterpieces won't be necessary after all.''

Rosa slipped out, half-shod, and disappeared through a side door.

Lissa checked herself in a mirror for telltale signs, saw streaks of plaster chalk on her green silk blouse and quickly shed it, glad of the T-shirt she wore under it. She put on her best "apologist" face and mounted the main staircase to the inn's third floor.

2

Wow! She came close to saying it aloud. Ginny's rave description hadn't prepared her for Steve Jackson. *Nothing* could have prepared her.

Six foot three if he was an inch, his tight, faded jeans riding low on lean hips, his broad chest bare except for a golden cloud of hair down its center... Lissa gulped. His shoulders nearly filled the doorway. Dark blond hair curled over his forehead, begging for a woman's hand to brush it back.

She fought down the urge to reach up, clenching her fists behind her while trying to look relaxed, professional, and concerned all at the same time.

The frosty glare faded from his blue eyes as his gaze swept over her in clear appreciation—and, she saw, speculation. He gave her a complete once-over—twice. From the top of her head, slowly down over her bosom, to her hips and her legs, now mercifully hidden by the fullness of her skirt. His gaze was so piercing, Lissa felt as if he could see through the gathers of the fabric. She caught her breath and spoke.

"Mr. Jackson?" she said, holding out her hand. "I'm Lissa Wilkins, night manager." A minor promotion wouldn't hurt her credibility, and after all, she was in charge tonight.

He took her hand, wrapping his around it. His grip was firm and his fingers and palm so callused it was obvious he was accustomed to doing hard work. Would the older son of a hotel magnate work so hard at anything? Suddenly, she wanted with a terrible intensity for Steve Jackson not to be who they thought he was.

But he had to be. The laws of coincidence stretched only so far and no farther.

"Hello, Lissa," he said, in a deep, husky voice that sent tingles down her spine. She gently pulled her hand free. Though they were at arm's length, she still detected a whiff of a spicy aftershave or maybe shampoo, and a malty odour of beer. Everything about him—his mesmerizing blue eyes, his tall, lean, muscular body and that sexy voice, plus the sensations his hands had produced were sending her into sensory overload.

He stepped back three paces. Like a dinghy in tow, she followed him into the room. With difficulty, she forced her gaze from his eyes to the mess on his bed.

Sure enough, there was that damned little steamer trunk spilled open, and blood was spattered all over his bedding.

There was no sign of Rosa's Birkenstock. Her knees went weak with relief. It must be in the attic. He had no proof that half a woman had ever been in his room.

"Oh, cripes," she said, casting a glance at the hole in the ceiling. "What a mess! Did the trunk strike you on the head? You must have lost a great deal of blood. Please, sit down."

Solicitously, she tried to steer him toward the one chair in the room. It was like trying to move a three-hundred-year-old cedar. Giving up, she asked, "Do you need medical attention? We don't have a doctor here in Madrona Cove, but I could get someone to run you to town and—"

"No." He firmly removed her hand from his arm,

the strength of his fingers effectively cutting off both her breath and speech.

"I don't need medical attention. I don't need to sit down. Nothing hit me in the head. The blood's from my nose, the result of that crazy woman kicking me."

"Woman?" Lissa made her eyes big and round. "Oh, yes. You mentioned a woman when you called downstairs. Where…um, where is she?"

He tilted his head back to stare at the hole. She watched him swallow before he turned to her. "I don't know." His brows drew together. "I couldn't pull her down, so I boosted her back up. At her request."

His eyes narrowed as he glanced at her. "I use the word 'request' loosely. She threw the trunk at me, then disappeared."

"Of course." Lissa nodded sympathetically. "This woman who disappeared threw the trunk at you." She smiled kindly. "Are you absolutely sure it didn't hit you on the head?"

"Yes, dammit, I'm sure! Listen, if you think I'm imagining the woman, I can give you details. She's wearing ugly brown leather sandals, has long legs, and some kind of bug tattooed on her butt. This is a small town. Doesn't that help you identify her?"

Lissa kept her face serene and her tone even. She prayed the tingle of heat she felt in her face didn't show as a betraying blush. "No, sir," she said. "Uh, you were at Chuckles this evening, I believe?"

He glared. "I am not drunk."

"Of course not, sir. I wasn't suggesting you were."

He hooked his thumbs through the belt loops of his low-slung jeans, his blue eyes narrowing to slits. "You sure as hell were."

"It's just that…" She shrugged helplessly and

worked up a consoling smile. "Well, sometimes people on vacation feel a little more relaxed than they normally do, and drink more than they intended and then begin to take some of the local legends too seriously, and—"

"Legends?" He snorted derisively. "Oh, you mean the ghost."

Feeling like an idiot, but knowing it was for a good cause, Lissa said, "I wouldn't dismiss her too lightly. She was my great-grandmother. She appears to some people or makes her presence known in other ways. Sometimes she laughs, though mostly she cries."

He gave her a skeptical grin. "Oh? Why?"

"Shortly after my great-grandfather, who built the inn, died, she lost one of the pearl earrings he'd given her for their tenth anniversary. She was distraught, and spent one long, rainy December night outside with a lantern, searching for it all over the grounds. She got pneumonia. The staff put her to bed—the family lived here on the top floor—and she continued wandering from room to room in delirium, trying to find that earring. She died, leaving her only child, my grandfather, an orphan. They say she's still searching for her earring."

She rubbed her arms as if a chill had run over her and looked over her shoulder. "I spent my summers in this very room, and I can tell you…odd things happen."

He bit his bottom lip for an instant, looking just a little uneasy. She had to struggle to keep a straight face.

"You own this inn?" he asked.

"My family used to," she said.

"My father owns several resorts," he said. "I don't think any of them are haunted."

Well! He was certainly up-front about what his father did. Maybe he didn't realize they all knew exactly why he was here.

"I can't swear the place is haunted," she said. "My dad insists the sounds are nothing more than the wind in the limbs of the arbutus tree the inn's named for."

"Madrona Inn is named for an arbutus tree?"

"*Madrona* is the Spanish name for the tree. This is one of the northernmost specimens on the coast, and one of the oldest, I think, judging by its size. You've seen it, I'm sure. The big, gnarled, twisted, red-barked tree outside the dining room? It comes right up to the windows on this floor and sometimes makes terrible noises when the wind blows. That's probably all you heard tonight." She hoped she'd managed to inject a note of doubt into her voice.

She smiled. "Also, if you've had a little more to drink than normal, things might not seem to be exactly as they are."

"I wasn't complaining about a ghost." He pointed one long, tan finger. "That trunk is exactly what it seems to be. So's the hole in the ceiling, and the crap all over my bed."

"Yes. Mmm-hmm. The trunk is certainly real."

"So," he said, his voice taut, "is my aching nose." He rubbed its bridge gingerly with two fingers. "The heel that kicked me didn't belong to any ghost."

His nose did look as if it had been broken—though not recently. Still, she had the most ridiculous impulse to kiss it better. *Get a grip,* she told herself. "Those darned termites," she said with concern. "Must have chewed clear through another beam. I hope we can make up to you for this…inconvenience." She shook her head in despair as she stared at the damaged ceiling.

Looking doubtful, he raised his thick brows. "Go on," he invited.

"Tonight, of course," Lissa said, "I'll move you to another room, and your stay to date will be on the house." Then, as inspiration suddenly struck her, she added quickly, "Tomorrow, I can try to book you into another resort."

Of course! Her dad, the whole committee, would be so proud of her. Her unfortunate fall through the ceiling could be turned to their advantage. Surely, Steve Jackson gone was a whole lot better than Steve Jackson merely uncomfortable and sending home bad reports.

"At this point," he said, "what I want is another room, preferably one with a firm mattress and an intact ceiling. Tomorrow I'll decide what I want to do. I've paid for three weeks in advance."

"I understand," she said calmly. "Naturally, your money will be refunded and if there's a discrepancy between our rate and that of the resort you move to, we'll make up the difference." If she had to make it up out of her own pocket, she'd do it.

Again, his gaze swept over her. "*If* I decide to leave."

If? Lissa bit back an exclamation and schooled her face as best she could while she nodded. So much for her inspiration. Clearly, he wasn't about to go along with her agenda. "Of course. Well, then, if you'd care to pack up your things, Mr. Jackson, I'll go downstairs and get the key to your new room.

"You may leave your toiletries in the bathroom if you wish. You'll be moving next door to the adjoining room. Please excuse me for just a few minutes. I'll be right back.''

She slipped out and closed the door behind her, then stood leaning on it while she collected herself.

What did he mean, *if* he decided to leave? Why would he want to stay? Now that she had the notion of getting rid of him, she couldn't see it happening any other way. But, he didn't appear willing to cooperate. Lissa squared her shoulders and headed back downstairs. Okay. She'd offered him an out. If he didn't take it, if he didn't leave tomorrow, Steve Jackson's so-called vacation was really going to get interesting.

As Lissa Wilkins left the room, Steve couldn't get her out of his mind. Her bright brown eyes and her dazzling smile had hit him somewhere deep and elemental. She was tall, slender, yet voluptuous, and irrationally he believed she was the one who'd fallen through the ceiling.

He frowned. If so, she'd made one damned fast recovery. She'd appeared minutes after the incident, unruffled, serene, and hadn't so much as blinked when he mentioned that tattoo. Nor was there so much as a single dark mahogany hair out of place in her long, thick French braid.

Still, those brown eyes had widened when he'd said, ''If I leave.'' However quickly she'd regained her composure, there had been that momentary reaction of pure dismay.

As if she *wanted* him to leave.

But why?

His frown deepened as he began opening drawers to dump things in his suitcase and duffel bag. Nah. It had to be his imagination.

A drawer jammed, and he slammed it with the heel

of his hand. After another slam, the drawer finally opened straight, but before he could reach in for anything, it slid smoothly shut. He stared at it, then slowly pulled it open again. This time it stayed that way and he emptied it quickly, keeping a wary eye on it. Then he reached for the next drawer down. It slid open before he so much as touched it.

He stared at it. This place was definitely weird.

The building was *old*. So, more than likely, the floor must have sagged when he shifted his weight, causing the drawer to open on its own. Still, he rushed through the rest of his packing, irrationally wanting out of that room.

He rolled aside the trunk on his bed to locate the T-shirt he'd shucked earlier, and uncovered one ugly brown sandal.

Holding it on the palm on his hand, he laughed softly. "Ah-*hah!*"

It was old and well-worn, with heel and toe marks clearly impressed in the sole. Ghosts didn't wear Birkenstock sandals. Here was irrefutable proof the woman existed.

But not proof enough that the woman was—or was not—Lissa Wilkins.

He had a mystery on his hands. A mystery and a challenge, neither of which he could resist. Who owned that sandal and why had she been in the attic directly over his bed?

In the meanwhile, he was looking forward to spending more time with Lissa, and learning more about her, and what she was up to.

When Lissa returned to take him to his new room, he was taken aback by the impact of her big brown eyes on him.

She gestured for him to precede her into the adjoining bedroom and he sauntered through the door, duffel over one shoulder, suitcase in the other hand, feeling her gaze on his back.

The room was larger than the one he'd just left. The bed—a genuine, antique sleigh bed, or his mother hadn't taught him one damned thing—appeared to have no sag in the middle.

"Ahhh..." he said, sitting on the edge of it, then flopping backwards. Good! The bed was antique, but the mattress was not, and was as firm as it looked. He smiled up at Lissa Wilkins, who stood with her hands behind her back, her eyes flickering below her thick lashes and a faint flush rising up her cheeks. "Too bad I wasn't assigned to this room in the first place. Then I wouldn't have such a mystery to solve."

"Oh?" Lissa said trying to sound nonchalant. She knew exactly what mystery he was talking about, and she didn't want him trying to solve it. She wanted him disturbed and uneasy and unable to find anything positive to say about the Madrona Inn. Even more, she wanted him gone.

"Who knows what lurks in the dark, dusty attic rooms of the Madrona Inn?" he intoned. "Who knows what manner of creature dwells in the shadows? Who knows when the pods will hatch and the aliens come crashing through the ceilings? Will they make their way from floor to floor, devouring everyone in their path, gaining strength with each new victim they consume? Will they—"

Lissa laughed. "Now I *know* that trunk hit you on the head! Is there anything else I can do for you, Mr. Jackson?"

He lay sprawled across the bed, his head propped on a pillow.

"I don't know." Idly, he patted the mattress as if in silent invitation. "What do you think?"

Lissa stared at the empty area of the bed. She would fit nicely beside him, next to his outspread arm. He'd have only to curl his arm and she'd roll up against his side and—

Lissa bit back a gasp. "Think?" she echoed.

"About what else you could do for me."

Nothing like this had ever happened to her—not in her teenage years working as a chambermaid, nor in the two years she'd been back at the inn. Suddenly she realized she was ill prepared to deal with a man like Steve Jackson. Especially while he lay on his bed, with a provocative smile on his face, as if he knew exactly how his teasing was affecting her. *If* he was teasing.

"Not a thing, Mr. Jackson." As she spoke, she turned to leave.

"How about a nightcap?" he asked. He rolled toward her and sat up.

"I'm sorry," she said, her hand on the doorknob. "The bar is closed."

"What a shame." He stood up, reached over and snagged her elbow.

"Then how about another bedtime story?"

She laughed. "Another what?"

"Well, the one about the ghost surely wasn't designed to lull me to sleep. Maybe you should try again."

She shook her head. "What I told you was no bedtime story, Mr. Jackson. I wouldn't know one of those if it bit me on the…ankle."

His hand slid from her elbow to her wrist, and suddenly his fingers were linked with hers. "Then how about *I* tell *you* one?" he said. "Or how about we act it out?"

He gently turned her around and, without knowing quite how she'd gotten there, she found herself seated in a chair. Still holding her hand, he crouched before her. With his free hand, he dragged his duffel bag closer, reached into it and pulled out Rosa's Birkenstock.

Lissa tried not to show her dismay. *Damn!* She'd been counting on that sandal still being safely in the attic, but here it was in Steve Jackson's big hand. He grasped her left ankle, trying to lift her foot from the floor. Lissa's breath caught in her throat.

"What do you think you're doing?" she said, keeping her foot firmly planted on the floor, resisting his efforts to lift it.

His grin flashed again. "I have this glass slipper— well, okay, leather sandal—and I aim to find my secret princess, the one whose foot will fit."

Lissa bit her lip.

"What do you think?" he asked. "There's a prize for the winner."

"How thrilling."

"You don't like prizes?"

"Depends on what they are."

"You'll have to try the sandal on for me if you want to find out."

"Let me guess," she said. "The prize wouldn't happen to be just over six feet tall and have blue eyes, would it?"

He puffed out his chest, struck a pose and—she fought the urge to laugh—batted his eyelashes. They were long and thick and definitely worth batting. "Oh-ho! The lady thinks I'm a prize!"

Her laughter escaped. "A prize idiot, maybe. You'd make a better Court Jester than a Prince Charming."

"Oh, you wound me!" he said.

"Too bad. If you're completely finished with this foolishness, I'd appreciate regaining custody of my foot. I was never very fond of the Cinderella story."

His fingers maintained a loose hold on her ankle. "No? What story do you like, Lissa?"

"Have you ever read *The Paper Bag Princess*, by Robert Munsch?"

He laughed. "No," he said. "I don't think I have."

"If you ever get a chance, I recommend it."

"Tell me the story yourself," he said, letting her go slowly, reluctantly, she thought, his fingers trailing down her ankle and the top of her foot until stopped by her shoe.

"Nope. You want a bedtime story, go ask your mommy."

"No maternal instincts, huh?"

She rose. "Not a single one."

"Maybe they just haven't developed yet," he said, and to her shock, tucked her arm, drawing her into the loose circle of his arms. Automatically, her hands went to his shoulders. "So I guess I'll have to settle for a good-night kiss."

She could have prevented it. She was certain she could have. She could have escaped with no trouble, except she wasn't sure her knees would support her weight unless she hung on.

His left hand rested on her waist, while his right pulled lightly on her braid, tilting her face up so she was looking into his eyes. What she saw there behind the laughter disturbed her, frightened her...and excited her, too.

When he dropped his head and brushed his lips over hers, a shudder rippled through her and she jumped back quickly. "No!"

He let her go easily, grinning. "Aw, darn. How come real life is never like fiction?"

"Maybe," she suggested, "because you read the wrong kind of fiction."

She slammed the door on her way out, and stomped down the hall. *Damn him!* Could he sense how easily he'd gotten inside her defenses?

Oh, of course he could! A man who looked like him? He knew exactly how to play a woman, just as well as most of the inn's other guests knew how to play a fish. *And,* she acknowledged as she marched down the stairs as quietly as she could, given her mood and her clogs, his flirtatiousness had one purpose, and one purpose only: he wanted to get a look at her bottom, to check for a tattoo.

Well, did she have news for him! Nobody, but nobody, got a look at her butt. Not anymore.

It was thanks to a man just like Steve Jackson, with sky-blue eyes, wide shoulders and muscular legs, that she had that particular "identifying characteristic" in the first place. She was an entire decade, and then some, past the stupid age of twenty when it had seemed a real hoot to get that tattoo—no thanks to Joe's persuasive powers and her having drunk too many Stingers. Getting the tattoo had hurt, but not as much as Joe had later hurt her.

If only she'd learned from her experience with Joe, but uh-uh, not her. It had taken Casey to reinforce the lesson, and Tony to make it stick. But now she knew:

a smart woman steered clear of any great-looking guy with more dangerous charm than a caravan of gypsies. Like Joe, Steve Jackson would undoubtedly have romantic duplicity on his mind.

From now on, she planned to stick to men who were over forty, balding, paunchy, and grateful simply to be noticed. That kind of man might not be exciting, but he'd be safe. And so would her heart.

Since her brainstorm of getting him to leave appeared doomed to failure, she'd just have to steer clear of Steve Jackson. According to the plan, it was up to Ginny to keep him entertained when he wasn't fishing.

There hadn't been a man created who could resist Ginny McKay if Ginny made up her mind not to be resisted. She'd been married once, disastrously, and swore she'd never try that again. Instead, she played the field, enjoying men's company, but refusing to take any of them seriously. Lissa had never known a happier, more self-confident woman than Ginny, and Steve Jackson didn't stand a chance.

Once the weather cleared and he was out on the water every day, and busy chasing Ginny at the bar in the evenings, he'd be sleeping like an exhausted child each night.

Except at around 1:30 and 3:30...

Which reminded her: she was going to have to get someone to reposition the equipment in the attic so it was right over his new room. There was no way she was going up there again. Once was more than enough, regardless of the stakes involved. There was any number of others on the committee who could do it. Larry, for one. He owned and operated the machine shop and marine ways, but there was no rule saying only an employee of the inn could plant the tapes. Larry was an

active member of the committee and like both Lissa
and Ginny, knew the inn inside and out, having played
hide-and-seek with them during their childhood.

If he couldn't do it, then there was Merv, the marina
manager. Merv had as much at stake as any of the rest
of them. A new owner might just as easily replace him
as keep him on and he was nearing fifty. He wouldn't
find it easy to get another job.

She'd put the problem to the committee at their Sunday morning meeting. Someone would do what was
needed.

Anyway, the seeds had been planted now. Even if
Steve Jackson didn't believe in ghosts now, he soon
would…

THIS WAS ONE HOT piano player for a small town, Steve
thought. He was sitting backward on a bar stool in
Chuckles the following evening, watching the Saturday-night entertainment. The guy almost made love to
his keyboard, lying half-across it as he played. The
woman with the fiddle wasn't bad, either, and the tall,
mostly bald guy with his remaining hair tied back in a
ponytail got more emotion out of a sax than anyone
he'd ever heard. The singer, Ginny, was back, and just
like the night before, he could have sworn she was
singing each word directly to him.

Larry Cranshaw, the man on the next barstool, noticed, too. "Cute, huh?" he said, giving Steve a poke
with his elbow.

Steve grinned at him. "Sure is."

He'd met Larry over the pool table a couple of days
ago and the two had hit it off immediately. A First
Nations man who claimed direct descendancy from the
great chief Maquinna, and whose chiseled face bespoke

his Nootka ancestry, Larry had lived in Madrona Cove all his life. He knew everyone.

"I think she's got the hots for you," he said. "Her name's Ginny McKay. She's divorced and lonely. Want an introduction?"

"Nah." Steve shook his head. Petite, redheaded and bosomy, Ginny was cute, all right. "We've met, actually. I'm staying at the inn." Ginny was also the hostess in the Madrona Inn's dining room.

"And?" Larry's face and tone expressed amazement. "You don't like her?"

"Sure. She's okay."

"Huh. Lots of guys think Ginny's more than okay. She's elusive. Friendly as all get-out, but simply won't be caught. People make book on when she'll finally succumb. They say it'll take a man in a million to capture her."

"Really," Steve said. It sounded to him as if Larry was almost daring him to take up the challenge.

"Yup. If I wasn't married, I might even give it a try myself." He hesitated. "You married?"

Steve shook his head. Larry arched one eyebrow. "So? Why not buy her a drink during her break? Get to know her a little better."

"I don't think so. Nothing against the lady," Steve added. "She's just not my type."

"Oh, yeah?" Larry looked interested. "What is?"

Steve shrugged. "Leggy. I like them leggy." He nodded toward one woman on the dance floor. "Like that." She had long, blond hair that swirled when her partner spun her around, and a short, full skirt that flared out. From his position on his bar stool, he thought her legs might be the pair he was seeking, but it was hard to be sure.

Larry laughed. "I don't recommend it. Her boy-friend's the meanest logger in town."

"Oh, yeah?" The leggy blonde's partner didn't look particularly mean. Or dangerous.

"Now there's another leggy one," Larry said, giving Steve another nudge with his elbow. "How about her?"

Steve followed the direction of Larry's gaze and saw Lissa standing with a group seated at a table. Before he could slip off his stool and amble on over toward her, one of the men, an older version of *Jeopardy* host Alex Trebek, slipped an arm around her waist and pulled her down onto his lap. She draped an arm around his shoulders and kissed his cheek, looking per-fectly at home.

"Yeah," Steve said, irritated beyond all reason. "*How* about her?"

Before Larry could point out any other possibilities to him, a woman slipped up to Larry's side and snug-gled her arm through his. "You going to sit here all night, or are you planning to dance?"

"Dance, I guess," Larry said with a grin. Then, to Steve, as if he owed him some kind of explanation, he added, "She's my sister-in-law." He led the woman onto the floor. Steve glanced at Lissa, who was now seated at the table, sharing a heaping plate of fish and chips with her companion. Steve turned away, but something kept drawing his eyes back to her. When he saw her pick up a slice of lemon from the plate and suck on it, his mouth puckered, but that wasn't his only response.

Annoyed, he sauntered toward the stage occupied by the musicians. Ginny McKay smiled at him so seduc-tively that he couldn't help smiling back. But he didn't want to encourage her, so he took a chair at the last empty table near the edge of the dance floor. From that position, he was completely unable to watch Lissa Wilkins making up to the older guy.

The long-legged blonde swirled by with her partner and obviously noticing his attention, gave him a flirtatious wink and a tantalizing glimpse of her thighs. But her skirt didn't go high enough for him to see if she had a tattoo. He slumped down as low as he could on his chair without sliding off or becoming too conspicuous, or both.

No good.

He needed to see more of her if he was to be sure. Briefly, he considered pretending to fall off his chair so he could look up her skirt, but that seemed unwise, especially for a guy who didn't want to be conspicuous.

When Lissa came dancing by in the arms of the gray-haired man, he nearly rose, whether to leave or to cut in, he couldn't have said, but in doing so, he accidentally tripped the blonde, who fell into his lap as he collapsed back into his chair.

He wrapped his hands around her waist and held her steady. "Whoa there! You all right?" Out of the corner of his eye, he saw Lissa circling to the far side of the dance floor, talking to her partner, a serious expression in her face. The man patted her cheek and kissed her nose.

"Sure, I'm okay," the blonde said, wriggling a little on his lap. "Just a bit dizzy. I guess I tripped over my brother's feet. He's never been much of a dancer." She giggled. Her eyes were such a glassy green he knew she'd had more than a little to drink. "Thanks for catching me."

"My pleasure," he said, setting her upright while

managing to slide one hand down over her hip and thigh, checking her size and shape. He concluded she was a tad too rounded, too padded.

Suddenly, a guy as big as a mountain loomed up. "Hands off, bub." His lantern jaw jutted out aggressively as he set two mugs of beer on the table with a single, ominous thump.

"Oh, Jase—honey, don't be like that," the woman said, patting his cheek. "The nice man was just trying to help after Ronnie tripped me. Right, Ron?" But Ron was standing at an adjacent table, drawing a pretty, pregnant woman to her feet.

"Just trying to help himself," the logger said through clenched teeth.

The last thing Steve wanted was a brawl over a woman, especially with Lissa Wilkins in the bar. "Hey, no offense," he said quickly. "Let me buy you a drink. Both of you. Name's Steve Jackson." He offered his hand to the huge man. After a narrow-eyed, suspicious moment, Jase took the hand and pulled one of those I-can-crush-you-like-an-eggshell grips on Steve, who smiled all the way through it.

He joined them and the other couple at their table. From there it was easy to see Lissa. When her date went to play darts, leaving her sitting with two other women, he rose, strolled in her direction and asked her to dance.

"Oh!" Lissa accepted with trepidation. Steve's hand was large and warm as he wrapped it around hers and led her toward the dance area. Luckily, the music was lively, and they could dance without touching—except that his gaze touched her. Even when she turned from him, spinning in time to the throbbing rock beat, she knew he was watching her, looking at her legs, encased tonight in tight jeans. She wished she'd refused Steve's invitation to dance, and when the band segued into a slow, sensuous tune, she wished she was at the bottom of the sea.

3

THE SONG WAS a real oldie, full of romantic phrases about moonlight and roses.

"You smell good," Steve said, brushing his face over her hair for just an instant, but it was an instant that made Lissa dizzy, forcing her to slide her arm a little higher on his shoulder so she wouldn't stumble.

She jerked her head back and met his gaze. "It's just shampoo," she said.

He smiled, slowly and sweetly and right into her eyes. "I don't think so. I think it's you." He drew her a little closer, until their thighs were brushing as they danced. It made it so easy to follow his lead, and she relaxed into the sensuous rhythm. Silent now, they circled the floor, keeping to the outer edges.

As they crossed in front of the bandstand, Ginny, letting the others carry the melody with the instruments, covered the microphone with one hand and leaned forward. "Lookin' good, Liss. Want to trade jobs?"

Lissa flicked what she hoped was a quelling glance at her friend, who winked and picked up the lyrics as if she'd never paused.

"Jobs?" Steve asked. "You sing, too?"

Lissa nearly choked. Damn that Ginny. Always sailing too close to the wind. It was just like her to give

Steve an opening like that, a reason to ask questions. "No!"

"No you don't sing, or no you don't want to trade jobs with her?"

"No to both."

He drew her even closer. "Good," he murmured, his breath fanning her ear. "I'd rather dance with you than with her." He slid his hand lower down on her back, pressing her to him. "You and I, we fit."

It was true. There was just enough height difference that she felt comfortable with him. *Too* comfortable. She wished the band would choose something else, something fast, something lively, something that would get her out of Steve Jackson's arms, get her far enough away from him that she could breathe without drawing in the scent of his body.

On their next pass near the stage she could ask Charlie, the pianist, to pick up the pace. Some Creedence Clearwater Revival material would be good. Charlie liked the old stuff, and Ginny was good at belting out "Lookin' Out My Backdoor."

Assuming Lissa was still breathing by then. Was she breathing now? She wasn't sure, but somehow it didn't matter. She was…feeling. Feeling too many things, her senses all tangled up and confused. They passed the stage. She couldn't have called out to Charlie any more than she could have stopped dancing with Steve as long as the music played. Music? Did she really hear it, or was that just her heartbeat roaring in her ears? Suddenly, she was afraid that it had stopped, and she was on the floor with Steve, swaying in time to a beat only the two of them could hear.

It wasn't until she had to force her eyes open that she realized they had been closed. She lifted her head off Steve's shoulder, unsure how it had ended up there, or how long it had been there, and cast a pleading glance at her best friend, as they danced near the stage.

"Chicken Dance," she managed to croak out, and could only hope Ginny had heard, had understood.

Thank goodness! Just before Steve spun her way from the stage, she saw Ginny turn and murmur something to Lorne, on the sax, who in turn spoke to Charlie.

She almost broke away from Steve, ready to stick her elbows out and start clucking, but then Ginny's voice softened, deepened, the saxophone moaned in a heartbroken sob, Charlie's fingers dropped an octave on his keyboard and Marsha's violin wept along with the sax.

"When I fall in love," Ginny sang, her mouth close to the mike, "it will be forever..."

Steve's breath fanned her hair, which, thanks to the exertion of their earlier fast dance, was escaping from the clip that held it back. Softly, he began to sing along. "'Or I'll never fall in love...'" He had a mellow voice, deep and throaty, and it seemed to seep through her pores, right into her soul. His arm across her back drew her closer, his hand holding hers tucked in between them. This was too much. It was too close, but she couldn't seem to break away. The world spun, whirled, went dark and soft around her.

"'And the moment I can feel that...'"

Suddenly she felt overwhelmed by the urge to cry. She squeezed her eyes shut, turned her face toward the center of Steve's chest in an attempt to escape the sound of his voice, the feel of his breath against her ear, and found all she'd accomplished was to put herself into even closer contact with him. She gave up and surrendered to the feelings, taking each moment as it came, reveling in it, allowing herself these few minutes out of a lifetime of whose emptiness, whose bleakness, she'd never been fully aware until now.

Slowly, tenderly, Ginny drew the song out to its very end. Then all that was left was the sweet melancholy of the last few notes Lorne wrung from his saxophone.

After a moment of complete silence, the dancers as well as the listeners around the bar began to applaud enthusiastically. Steve released Lissa's numb body. He, too, applauded. She tried to lift her hands, but it was all she could do to simply keep herself upright on the floor.

"We'll be takin' a little break now," Ginny said into the microphone, and the dancers slowly left the floor. For a moment Lissa thought she'd be unable to move. Then her dad came up behind her and Steve.

"It's 10:30, honey," he said. "You ready to go?"

Weakly, she nodded. She managed to lift her gaze to Steve's and murmur, "Good night," before her father slid his arm over her shoulders and she wrapped hers around his waist for support.

The cooler, rainy air outside brought her back to her senses and she drew in several deep breaths of it. "Thanks for dinner, Dad. I'd better go down to the boat and get ready for work."

"Yup," he said, kissing her cheek again. "See you tomorrow? The meeting's at ten."

"I'll be there," she said, then watched him walk away into the night.

"But tonight," she added to the dark sky, "is absolutely the last time I'll be *here*. At least until Steve Jackson has gone."

What in the world had come over her? She'd danced

with him as she'd never danced with another man before, not even when she was young and foolish and thought every fleeting emotion she felt must be true love. She was older now, and a heck of a lot wiser. Wise enough to recognize that the wild sensations Steve had created in her had another name—lust.

But lust was something she could control. All it took was a little self-discipline and a lot of remembering the trouble it could get a girl into. There was only one way to deal with a man like him: from a distance. A very, very long one.

YEAH, RIGHT. "Time to go, honey" and off she went, just like that, Steve thought, watching Lissa go off with the gray-haired man. What the hell! Hadn't she felt any of the things he'd felt? Hadn't she understood exactly how right they'd been together? Not only in size, but in mood. They'd felt the same things, heard the same words, taken the same meaning from those songs. He could have sworn to it. But then her gray-haired boyfriend had stepped right in, and in a flash she was gone with him, her arm draped affectionately around his waist.

What the hell did the old guy have that Steve didn't? Hah. Stupid question. What did most old guys who attracted young women have? Moola, bread, liquid assets, whatever you wanted to call it. And what was he? A currently unemployed commercial diver. Big deal.

He stomped to the bar and got himself another beer, sat down on a stool and watched the dancers. There she was again, that leggy blonde. Sitting down, the big bruiser nowhere to be seen.

Sure. Why not? Carrying his beer, he crossed the

dance floor, weaving his way between gyrating couples, and set his glass on her table.

"Dance?" he said, determined to wash away the memory of the way Lissa Wilkins had felt in his arms. It had been a fluke, of course. Any woman would have felt that way to him, after his long dry spell.

She smiled up at him, her eyes even glassier, and hopped nimbly to her feet. She might be a bit tipsy, but it didn't stop her shaking her bootie at him. He grinned, snapping his fingers, encouraging her.

Okay, maybe he shouldn't have encouraged her quite so enthusiastically. Maybe he should have tried to stop her when she jumped onto a chair, then onto an empty table, where she spun so fast her skirt flew up around her waist, but he didn't.

All it earned him, though, was a fist grabbing the back of his collar, another holding the back of his belt, and a rapid trip out the door, his feet crunching and splashing in the rain-soaked gravel of the parking lot. Then all six-foot-three, two-hundred-odd humiliated pounds of him was shoved up hard against the tailgate of a muddy pickup.

Jase had at least three inches in height, six in reach, and forty pounds of heft over Steve. Even if he hadn't been so badly outgunned, however, he wouldn't have wanted to make an issue of it. Not once he'd gotten a good, hard look at the blonde's nether regions, prettily displayed by her very high-cut black bikini briefs, and discovered there was no tattoo low on her left cheek. So he just apologized to Jase, and with another shove, Jase let him go on his way.

He crossed the potholed road to the inn. A middle-aged woman whose face bespoke sore feet or an aching back stood behind the front desk where Steve had hoped to find Lissa. She looked at him as if he were Jack the Ripper reincarnated, and he quickly turned away from her before her glare turned him to stone. In the lounge, a bored bartender polished glasses while overseeing three elderly couples. Two couples played cards at one table, while the third appeared embroiled in a rousing game of Scrabble.

The male Scrabble player rose unsteadily and tottered toward Steve.

"Hey. You the man on the top floor?"

Steve hesitated, then nodded.

"A little less noise tonight, if you please. My wife and I are both eighty-seven years old and have been coming here for fifty years. We've never been subjected to such shenanigans. We need our sleep. All that carrying on, crashing and banging—there's no excuse for that kind of behavior in a nice place like this. You want rowdy, you stay in that den of iniquity across the street. You got that, sonny?"

Steve bit back a smile. Chuckles, a den of iniquity? But then, compared to the Saturday-night crowd in the Madrona Inn, maybe it was. Solemnly, he apologized, but offered no explanation.

As he headed up the stairs, he heard a quavery little female voice say, "Good for you, Harry. These youngsters need..." The rest was lost as he rounded the corner of the landing. *Need what? Discipline?* he wondered. *A good talking to once in a while?* He chuckled. It was a long time since he'd thought of himself and his contemporaries as "youngsters." Still, he supposed to eighty-seven, thirty-seven might seem almost young.

Well, maybe the old man had a point. As he flopped down on his bed, he felt like a sophomore who'd just seen the cute girl taken away by the senior football hero.

And he wasn't thinking about the blonde.

The sound of creaking footsteps jerked Steve out of a deep sleep. He rubbed his eyes and sat up in his bed and stared up at the ceiling. Was the sound coming from the attic?

No. It seemed to be coming from his closet. His heart beating fast, he heard what sounded like wire hangers, rattling, clanking together then...there was nothing. Moments later, an even odder sound came from the closet. He sat very still, staring at its door. Slowly, he got to his feet and flung it open. Inside, his pants, shirts and jackets, neatly arranged on hangers, which he had hung from the right side of the closet, had mysteriously moved to the left side.

He scowled, wondering if the old inn had sunk a couple of inches on one side in the past few moments, causing his hangers to slide. But no. New buildings settled. Any settling in this old stone-and-wood structure had long since taken place. The bar in the closet appeared perfectly level.

Carefully, he moved his clothing back to the right side of the closet and shut the door. He was halfway across the room when he heard the hangers moving again. This time, he lunged at the closet and jerked it open in time to see his clothing back on the left, still swaying slightly, the few empty hangers clinking gently together. He returned everything to where he wanted it and backed away. Leaving the closet door open, he sat on the edge of his bed and waited. And waited some more. But nothing happened. Finally, convinced that whatever weirdness was going on in the room had finished for the night, he prepared for bed, turned out the light, and lay down.

His eyes could only have dropped shut for a second or two when he heard a distinctive sound of metal hangers sliding on a wooden bar. He flung himself out of bed, and flicked on the light. His clothes were back on the left, still swinging just a bit.

"All right. Fine. Stay there," he said, slamming the closet door.

Sleep was the last thing on his mind now. He dragged on a pair of jeans and a T-shirt, and left his room.

Glancing at his watch he saw it was nearly one o'clock. Maybe he'd find a little distraction downstairs in the lobby. He grinned in anticipation. Like maybe behind the front desk.

He was in luck. The sour-faced woman was gone, as were the bartender and the guests from the lounge, and Lissa was on duty, working at a computer. She glanced over her shoulder, met his gaze with a startled stare, and made two quick keystrokes that cleared her screen before he was close enough to see what was on it. He had the uncanny sensation that for just an instant, she had had a guilty expression. What had she been doing?

Guilty expression or not, she looked cool and un-ruffled, just as she had the previous night. Her hair was pulled back into that tidy braid, and she'd changed from her jeans into a chocolate brown long skirt with pink swirls, topped by a pink blouse. There was a slight flush in her cheeks as she rose, and a slight tremor in her hands, which she quickly tucked behind her.

"Hello, Mr. Jackson." She came to her side of the long desk and offered him a distant smile. Right now she was a far cry from the warm woman who'd melted into his arms while they danced, the woman whose brown eyes and moist lips had tempted him beyond all reason. If the other guy hadn't whisked her away, he'd have danced with her all night, even after the band quit. The dance she made him want to do didn't require any music.

"How's your ceiling holding up this evening? Any falling objects?" She grinned. "Or fallen women? You do seem to attract them, don't you?"

"Are you referring to yourself?" he teased.

"I was referring to Caroline Newson falling onto your lap."

"You can hardly blame me for that."

"Blame? I wasn't blaming you. I hope you enjoyed your evening."

"Parts of it," he said, leaning on the counter. "Some a whole lot more than others. How about you?"

She gave him a cool smile. "Some parts more than others. What can I do for you, Mr. Jackson?"

He cleared his throat. "Call me Steve, for one thing."

She clasped her hands together in front of her. "All right. What can I do for you, Steve?"

"I, uh, can't sleep."

"I'm sorry to hear that." She didn't say, "And what do you expect me to do about it?" but the implication was there in her tone. Laughter—or mockery—lurked in her brown eyes, ready to bloom at any second. Okay, so she wanted him to believe she hadn't experienced any of the things he had during those two close, slow dances. But he didn't believe her. Not for a minute. However, the reason for her pretense intrigued him.

"It's worry," he improvised, as if she'd asked the

cause of his insomnia. "About things falling through the ceiling on me. Mind if I visit awhile?"

"Have a cinnamon roll," she said, sliding a tray of pastries toward him. "Or an apple, an orange." A basket of fruit always sat on the counter, along with a tray of desserts from which guests could help themselves. "Maybe you're just hungry. A little snack might help you sleep."

He leaned on the counter. "I doubt it." He grinned and lowered his voice suggestively, intending to remind her of that good-night kiss he'd stolen yesterday. "But I know what would."

He loved the way she rose to the bait. Her chin came up and her eyes flashed. "So do I," she snapped.

"Yeah? What?" he asked.

"A cup of hot milk," she said sweetly, startling a laugh out of him.

"Hell! I expected something like: 'A two-by-four between the eyes.'"

"Would you like me to get you one?" she asked, her face deadpan, but her eyes flickering with humor.

"A two-by-four?"

She hesitated just long enough to suggest serious deliberation—and replied with a note of regret in her voice. "No, just hot milk."

"That kiss you gave me worked pretty well last night."

"I didn't *give* you that."

"Didn't you?" he asked, propping his elbow on the desk and placing his chin on his hand.

"Ooh," she said in a mocking tone. "I bet a hundred women have told you that makes you look sexy."

"At least a hundred," he agreed. "Does it?"

"Absolutely not," Lissa said, barely controlling her

laughter. Steve straightened as the outer door swung open and three men strolled in. They were George, Jamie and Mark Fredricks, a father and grown sons, who shared one of the inn's big, round dining tables with Steve and the Allendas, a pair of middle-aged sisters from California.

The men were laughing uproariously and were obviously three sheets to the wind, having clearly had too much to drink at Chuckles. "Hi, Liss," they chorused, letting the door slam loudly despite the hour.

"You really met your match tonight, didn't you, Steve?" George said, with a boisterous laugh. "Gotta hand it to you, though. You managed to stay on your feet. A guy'd think you got thrown out of bars every night."

Steve glanced at Lissa who was grinning. Under other circumstances, it might have been a captivating sight.

"You got thrown out of Chuckles?" He detected a certain awe, though probably not respect, in her voice.

"I merely got...hurried on my way," he said. "I was leaving anyhow, having accomplished my mission."

Her brown eyes widened. "Which was?"

"A real good look at Caroline's legs," George supplied, swiping at the tray of cinnamon rolls, missing, then staggering back for another, more successful try. "Jase was the one who hurried him on his way," he explained to Lissa before taking a large bite. "What a sight! You shoulda been there. One minute Caroline was dancing on the table and Steve here was holdin' her hand, the next, he was runnin' out the door with Jase holding him on tiptoe."

He gulped down a bite of his roll, turned to Steve

and added, "That Jase, he's one *big* guy, ain't he? Took guts, asking Caroline to dance, let alone putting her up on a table." He hiccuped.

"Thanks, George," Steve said dryly, making a mental note to talk loudly at breakfast and clatter cutlery against china, because George was sure to have a very sore head. He owed George for this. Lissa hadn't needed any more excuses to laugh at him.

"I didn't put Caroline on the table," Steve said, but Lissa merely looked at him as if unsure why he'd bothered offering her the denial. He wondered, too, and turned to watch the younger men tote their staggering father away. When he turned back they'd disappeared at the first landing, Lissa had a series of sketches spread out on the front desk, and was making notes on one of them. Each page depicted a medieval looking scene, complete with characters in costume.

"What's this?" he asked.

She glanced up. "The plan for this year's festival."

"Madrona Madness. Everyone's talking about it. The woman in the hardware store said it's your baby."

"Hardly," she said. "Lots of people work on it, Debbie included." At his questioning look, she explained, "Deb's the woman in the hardware store."

Steve wondered what it would be like to live in a place where everyone knew everyone else, and where there was only one hardware store, which was also the video store, the liquor store and post office.

"I'm just the coordinator," Lissa said with a shrug. "I take other people's ideas and pull them together."

He didn't think for a minute that was all. Besides, he wanted to keep her talking. He liked watching her animated face. "And?" he said. "What else?"

Again, she shrugged. "Well, I organize the different

booths, assigning spaces, making sure all our exhibitors and vendors have what they need to make the weekend a success. The theme this year is Fairy Tales and Legends.''

He joined her behind the front desk, leaned forward and read some of the titles written in the sketches. "Sherwood Forest?"

"It's where the archery contest will be run. My dad's in charge of that, which is great, because it's the first time in a long while he's taken an interest in the festival."

Steve heard happiness bubbling just under the surface of her tone, saw it shining in her eyes. She was close to her father, he surmised, with an unexpected surge of envy. "Why's that?"

"He had a stroke a couple of years ago and for a long time didn't take much of an interest in anything. His enthusiasm this year tells me he's pretty much recovered, which is good because—" She broke off so suddenly he was surprised she didn't bite her tongue.

"Because?" he prompted.

She shrugged and looked away. "Because who wants their father to be ill?"

He had to admit she had a point, but something told him there was more to it than what she was willing to divulge. But what the hell. It wasn't really his business, was it?

"I see this is labeled 'Jousting Field'," he said. "But it looks to me like it's in the water."

"It is." She looked up at him, smiling. "We hold it at high tide."

"How do the horses feel about that?"

Her laughter filled the air. "No horses, just logs and pike-poles. We're simply calling our usual log-rolling contest a jousting tournament in keeping with the theme."

"Log rolling! Great. I haven't seen one in ages. Not since I was about so high," he said, leveling off his hand at waist-height. "I used to think I'd like to try it."

"We have some pretty good contestants."

He figured she was warning him off. "And this?" he said, pointing to a semi-circle of rectangles that took up a good portion of the upland area.

"The exhibitors' booths." She picked up a sketch that depicted a small, open-fronted building with what looked like a thatched roof. "We won't use real thatch, of course, just a front with straw showing to give that impression. We want it to look as if we've created a marketplace in a castle courtyard."

"My first impression of Madrona Cove was that it was like stepping into a time-warp."

She grinned. "A wet one. It rained a lot the first few days you were here, didn't it?"

He smiled back at her. "Rain doesn't bother me. I explored. It's a quaint town, with those little houses perched on crooked little ledges at the water's edge, connected by all those stairs and boardwalks."

"I know," she said. "I love Madrona Cove mostly because it's changed so little since I was a child—since my great-grandparents first came here, really."

"It must be nice, having that kind of stability in your life, nothing much changing from your infancy to adulthood. Do you think your great-grandparents would see many differences, if they could come back?"

Her laughter was soft, almost teasing, and left him feeling as if a warm wind had just blown over him. "I hope so," she said, "or all the Madrona Madness celebrations we've had over the years would have been for nothing. During my dad's childhood, the community earned the money to buy the land where the park is. Since then, we've built a new library, a swimming pool and rec center, and now this year—"

She broke off, dropped her gaze to the floor as one of her sketches fluttered down.

He picked it up but didn't return it. "Now?" he prompted her, knowing she hadn't forgotten the subject, but was, for some reason, evading it.

She shrugged. "Whatever this year's fundraising is used for."

"Which will be?"

If she'd looked wary a moment ago, now she looked downright trapped. Then, as if making some kind of mental transition, she lifted her chin, squared her shoulders, and met his gaze head-on. "The purpose varies from year to year, but it always benefits the community."

He frowned. *What was so difficult about telling me that?* Instead of asking, he said, "How are those funds raised?"

"People rent booths to sell things. Visitors come from all over to attend the festival," she said. "They camp, stay aboard their boats, some even fly in and book hotel or bed-and-breakfast rooms for miles around. The population of Madrona Cove quadruples for that weekend. We really need a bigger park to hold them all. Of course, the more visitors we get, the better we like it since we get a percentage of sales for the community fund, in addition to rent.

"Then, we have the community sponsored events. They don't rent booths, but all their earnings go into the fund. Like the dunk tank, er, I mean the witch dunking stool, and—''

He laughed, interrupting her. "Witch dunking stool?"

"In a manner of speaking." He liked the sparkle in her eyes. A second later he didn't like the way she was eyeing him, though, as if sizing him up to see what kind of splash he'd make. "It's what we're calling it this year, in keeping with the Medieval theme."

"Who gets dunked?"

"Anyone who volunteers to get soaked fully clothed."

"You have people selling things, you have contests, you have games. I've got a great idea. Will you rent me a booth?"

A frown creased her brows. "What for?"

He dropped to one knee before her. "I'm thinking of running a Cinderella search."

She stared down at him and clutched the edge of the desk as he took her warm bare foot in both hands. Her eyes widened. "Really? And what would that entail?"

He stroked his finger from her heel to her toes. It was a very appealing foot. Funny, he'd never taken much notice of feet before. But then, he was a leg-man, and while feet belonged on legs, until this week, he hadn't spent much time thinking about them. Or looking at them. Or touching them. But he wanted, quite badly, to stroke Lissa's foot, cuddle it on his lap, play with her pink toes, kiss the arch and—

He stopped himself, knowing what painful and un-relieved physical response he was going to suffer if he didn't. "Discovering my secret princess," he said.

"Seems to me," she retorted, "we've had this con-versation before. So I suggest you get up off your knees before you do something really dumb, like proposing. That's what happened the last time a man got on his knees in front of me.''

"And did you accept?" he asked, his voice breaking slightly.

"What do you think?" she said. "I was twenty years old. The man was on his knees, for heaven's sake. He had a diamond ring in a little blue box. Of course I accepted.''

He had to laugh, and suddenly a tension he hadn't been fully aware of, snapped. She seemed to have a knack for doing that to him. Feeling stupid, he hauled himself back to his feet. "Oh, well, yes, I can see how that would force an acceptance out of you.''

He ran a thumb over her ringless fingers. Touching Lissa Wilkins was like walking on hot coals. Because he didn't believe for one second he could do it without getting burned, he likely would.

"What happened to him?"

"I haven't the faintest idea," she said, slipping her hand free. "We were engaged for something like three months. He liked the chase and the proposal so much he did it three or four times a year with three or four different women. He finally got all tangled up with too many fiancées and ended up with none.''

"You don't seem terribly heartbroken."

She flicked him with a teasing glance. "At the time, I was devastated—or thought I was. But proposals and engagements and breakups just seemed to keep happening to me over and over again until I got used to it. I got myself engaged a total of six times between the ages of twenty and thirty. Now, I know better.''

So that meant she wasn't engaged to the man whose lap she'd sat on.

"What?" he said. "You mean if a guy ever proposes again, he gets an automatic No? Is that what you'd say if I proposed?"

Her laughter, warm and musical, seemed to wash over him like the touch of soft, stroking fingers. "I'd probably ask you if another trunk had fallen on your head."

"No trunk ever fell on my head," he reminded her, unable to resist stroking her cheek with the tips of his fingers. "But I seem to be going a little bit crazy anyway. At least where you're concerned. I have a feeling that if I hang around here too long I just might find myself doing exactly that."

Her eyes widened. "Exactly what?"

"Proposing to you."

He couldn't tell who his statement surprised more, her...or himself.

"Then I suggest you don't hang around too long." Giving him the cold shoulder, Lissa exited into the back office. He shrugged, wondering what had gotten into him.

When he got back to his room, all his clothes were back neatly on the right of the closet and every one of his dresser drawers was open. As he watched, they closed silently, one by one. *She's searching for that earring...* A chill swept over his body.

"There's no such thing as ghosts," he said, but the words echoed hollowly in the room. Did he, or did he not, hear a hint of faint, faraway laughter?

Not. Absolutely, positively not.

4

"No way. Forget it!" Lissa stood with her hands on her hips surveying the gathering of committee members in her father's small trailer. "That's Ginny's job!"

"But he doesn't even like me," Ginny said.

"That's crazy. Men always like you!"

"Phil didn't."

"I thought you divorced him, not he you."

"Sure. But I divorced him because he didn't like me. He wanted me to be something I wasn't cut out to be—a corporate wife. Never marry a lawyer, Lissa."

"Don't worry. I have no intention of marrying anyone."

"Girls, girls, knock it off." Rosa thumped on the table with the bottom of her empty glass. "Nobody's asking you to marry the man, Liss, just, well, like your dad said, sort of make up to him, be nice. Keep him busy, off balance, and out of his room so the guys can do things."

"What things?" Lissa asked. "Aren't mysteriously opening and closing drawers enough? And when Larry gets the tapes properly positioned in the attic—by the way, Larry, thank you for offering to do that. No way was I going up there again with the spiders. Anyway, when he gets them up and running again, Mr. Jackson will take one night of ghostly wails and be out of here."

"I don't think so." Reggie shook his leonine head and folded his big, work-worn hands around his coffee mug. "I talked to him today and he doesn't come across like a guy who scares easy. And he doesn't believe in ghosts."

"So what good is it going to do, doing 'stuff' in his room?" Lissa asked in exasperation.

"One of these nights," Reggie said, grinning, "his bed just might collapse. Once my ankle's better, there's all sorts of things I can do to earn my keep as handyman."

"Not on your life!" Lissa's father said vehemently. "You harm that bed, mister, and you're in big trouble!" He really loved his grandparents' old furniture and couldn't understand why everyone else, Lissa included, didn't see each piece as the valuable artifact he did.

"I was joking, Frank," Reggie said patiently.

"Good thing, too," Lissa said, "Or Steve Jackson would be calling downstairs for me to do something about it."

"Which you wouldn't be able to," Reggie said. Reggie liked to think, and might have been right, that without his skills, the inn would have long since disintegrated.

"Hmm." Lissa considered it. "Maybe we *should* collapse his bed, then. I've already wrecked his first room. The lack of a bed in his second one might force him to pack up and leave."

"Maybe so," her dad replied, "but our purpose will be better served by keeping him here and making his stay uncomfortable."

How? Lissa was about to ask, when Rosa broke in, taking the idea one step further. "I could serve him the worst breakfasts I can come up with. Burned bacon, cold toast, watery eggs. And Jock," she went on, grinning at the red-headed dinner cook, "if you'd make a point of ruining his dinners, that would help. Lunch, being buffet, we can't do much about."

"We have to look at the big picture here," Frank interjected. "We have to accept the fact that we might fail. If we do, do we want Jackson Resorts Incorporated mad at the whole staff? Do we want Steve Jackson, in particular, mad at us? No," he answered for himself. "Because if we don't come up with the money this year, and our bid is lost, we might need him on our side. Who better to influence Jackson Senior than Jackson Junior?"

"I guess you have a point," Reggie admitted, scratching his head. "If we do lose out, we don't want to ruin our only chances of getting jobs in whatever kind of place Jackson Resorts puts in here."

"Do you honestly believe for one minute that he'd hire locals if he puts in a big, splashy modern resort?" Lissa asked. "I think we can forget that. Historically, it hasn't been done."

"Which is why, since we've been forewarned, we have an advantage no one else had," her father argued. "And getting Steve Jackson on our side can only add to that advantage. Lissa, you're the one who has the most to gain in this. After all, it's your heritage we're talking about here. Inn keeping's in your blood. If the town owns the inn, when I retire for good, you can become manager. Right, everyone?"

Everyone nodded.

Lissa bit back a groan. Her father knew perfectly well Madrona Inn wasn't a heritage she wanted any more than she wanted her great-grandparents' musty old junk. He knew, too, that she had other plans for her life.

"It's *your* heritage, Dad, not mine," she said firmly. "And that's why we're not going to fail. I know how much you want it, and I'm sure this summer's festival will put us over the top. When the town owns the inn, and appoints you manager again, we'll be home free."

"Then you'll do it?" he said, clearly seeing her words as capitulation. "I mean, keep Steve Jackson sweet and in a good mood? Make him like us as a community?"

"No," she said, jumping to her feet. "Oh, I'll be polite, I'll be friendly, the same as I would with any other guest, but that's as far as it goes. Now, if you'll all excuse me, I'm out of here."

She was tired from the sleep she'd lost the night before, thanks to Steve Jackson. She had a million things to do with the festival only two weeks away, and she wouldn't have time to keep him occupied.

Nor did she have the inclination. The sooner everyone believed that, the better off she'd be.

But, one of the hardest parts, she realized, might be convincing herself....

DAMN! There they went again, his dresser drawers, opening and closing, one after the other. And just when they settled down, the clothes in his closet began their nightly migration. That, Steve knew, could go on for the better part of an hour. Over the past two nights, he'd discovered that even if he left his hangers where he thought they wanted to be, within minutes, they'd change their minds. Jeez! What was he thinking? Hangers didn't have minds. And if this kept up many more nights, he wouldn't have one, either. He was even beginning to hope there *was* a ghost, after all. At least then he'd have an explanation for all this.

He sighed with frustration as the hangers started to shake, rattle and slide.

He needed some peace and quiet and rest. He certainly wasn't going to get it here in his room listening to hangers slide back and forth on the closet rod. He got out of bed, dressed and headed downstairs.

To his disappointment, there was no sign of Lissa in the lobby. On the front desk stood a little brass bell with a long, slender handle, just back of a sign saying Ring for Service. If he did, would she come running down the stairs, all flushed and breathless from having to hurry away from whatever she was doing to make his room appear haunted? Or would she come from that back room she'd disappeared into early Sunday morning when he'd made such a fool of himself? If she did, would she be tousled from sleep?

Did she have to stay awake all night when she was on duty, or did she simply have to be on the premises and available?

He thought about ringing the bell—after all, he owed her an apology. His joke about proposing to her had been completely out of line. No wonder she'd walked away from him and shut the door in his face. In the two days since then, he'd seen nothing of her. An apology was best given as soon as possible, he knew. So he really should ring that bell and get her out there where he could talk to her. But not if she was sleeping.

He turned from the desk and wandered down into the lounge where there were plenty of comfortable chairs and sofas. He'd sit down here and read till he was damn good and tired. Hopefully then, the odd go-ings-on in his room wouldn't keep him awake. Nothing would.

He tried reading his book for a while. It still didn't grab him so he picked up a magazine. While leafing through it, he stopped suddenly at a shampoo ad. He smiled.

The woman in it, her back to the camera, had long, molasses-colored hair, thick and sleek as he remembered Lissa's was when released from her braid the night they had danced. The model's hands and arms were raised, lifting the hair from her nape, letting it cascade down over her shoulders and back. It looked silky.

He could almost imagine smelling it, almost imagine stroking the smooth strands.

He imagined Lissa, sitting at a dressing table, brushing her hair. He would approach quietly, slip up behind her, take the brush from her hand. Slowly, gently, he'd run it through her thick tresses. He'd let them slide over and through his fingers, fall loose on his wrists and arms. The scent of her shampoo would rise to engulf him with its sweetness as he massaged her scalp. She'd sigh, lean back against his chest and tilt her head on his shoulder. He'd turn her half-around and lower his head toward her welcoming lips and taste them fully for the first time....

Leaning his head back, he closed his eyes, letting the fantasy play out.

Under her nightgown, her breasts, firm and round, would fill his hands with their warmth and heaviness. He would tip her back over his arm, then bend and take one of those delicious globes in his mouth, hearing her soft moan of pleasure and her voice encouraging him, telling him to take what he wanted because she was his, she belonged to him, she would do anything for him.... Don't stop, *she'd beg.* Don't ever stop, *and he would promise her he never would and tell her in graphic detail all the things he was going to do to her, while she whispered* yes, yes, yes, *to each one....*

LISSA TOSSED on the narrow cot in the back room where she spent a few hours of the night whenever she had a chance. She punched her pillow, turned it over and tried to find a cool spot on it.

Why wasn't she sleeping? Dammit, she knew why. She knew it all too well. In her head was a vision of Steve Jackson's hands, large and square and warm on her back, his body cradling hers, his thighs against hers and the sound of his voice, a low rumble, singing to her just as he had the night they'd danced together.

Did he sing to every woman he danced with? Who was she kidding? Of course he did! She knew that. It was his style. It was the style of all the men just like him she'd ever met, and she'd met plenty. Too many. Too many, at least, to be losing sleep over the guy.

She only wished Larry had got the tapes all set up as he'd promised, but when a big powerboat with a bent propeller had limped into his marine machine shop, he'd been tied up with work about fifteen hours a day. Then Janie, his wife, arrived home on this evening's ferry after a week at her grandmother's, and Larry had naturally had other things on his mind. Tomorrow, he'd promised. Tomorrow, the tapes would be in position.

She flopped on her back. At least she'd been spared the task of keeping Steve occupied since her dad and the committee had asked her to do it. Yesterday, he'd gone fishing with the Allenda sisters, and today, he'd gone out on his own, according to Merv, the marina manager. That suited her just fine. As long as he was fishing, he was out of her jurisdiction.

If he went fishing again tomorrow, and Larry had no emergency jobs come in, the tapes would be in place by noon.

The cot felt lumpier than it usually did. Her pillow was too thin. The sheet tangled around her bare legs so she had to fight to get rid of it. Heat seemed to have baked into the stone walls all day and was now being released into this small room. If she couldn't sleep now for thinking of Steve Jackson in his bed on the top floor, then she'd sleep tomorrow aboard her boat while he was out fishing, something at which she'd truly hate to join him.

She sat up quickly and flung her legs over the side of the bed. Not that she'd really like to join him upstairs, either, but well, a girl couldn't always control her mind's fantasies.

However, the reality was that she wasn't going to sleep any time soon. Fine. She'd go into the lounge and try to read some more of that big, boring book on medieval times. Not that it had given her a lot of ideas for the festival. She'd done better with the picture book of fairy tales she'd checked out of the library at the same time…along with *The Paper Bag Princess,* a mistake, because she hadn't known what it was, but a serendipitous one, because she'd enjoyed it so much.

She laughed softly. Now there was a princess with attitude: the right kind of attitude, one she could relate to—and would do well to emulate.

She rose, pulled on a skirt, straightened her scoop-neck cotton knit top and tidied her hair as best she could without rebraiding it. Then she went to the desk, hefted the big book of medieval times, all without bothering to turn on a light.

A light shone in the lounge and just as she was about to enter, she came to an abrupt halt, taken aback by the sight of Steve sitting quietly in a chair, his bare feet on a coffee table, a magazine on his lap.

He was completely unaware of her presence, so she took the opportunity to study him, trying to figure out just what it was about him that attracted her so strongly when every bit of good sense told her to steer clear.

Oh, he was a sexy devil, all right, and bantering with him had been fun. How long was it since she'd met a man who excited her, amused her, entertained her as much as he did? Too long, obviously, because she was way too interested in him.

She found herself wishing the light from the lamp at his side didn't cast such a golden glow over his hair and skin.

If only he'd go away!

He shifted slightly and she hoped he wouldn't look in her direction. His head began to nod, the magazine fell to the floor, and he lolled sideways against the back of the chair.

Sleeping! In the lounge! Now what was she supposed to do?

One thing, obviously. Her duty as night clerk demanded she march over there, grab his shoulder, shake him hard and wake him up. Send him back up to his room. Guests weren't supposed to sleep in the lounge, for Pete's sake! Pete. Right. All she needed was for Pete Hoskins, the manager, to make one of his rare surprise inspections and find Steve sleeping down here with her on duty. Pete didn't like her and would take any good excuse to get rid of her. She was lucky he'd never heard of the ceiling episode. Not that he'd have cared about the damage; Pete had, through managerial inaction, allowed the inn to deteriorate more in the two years of his tenure than all the absentee owners had throughout the years of her grandfather's and father's management. Sometimes, she thought it was almost willlful neglect, as if he wanted to see the inn tumble into the ocean.

Maybe it was time for them to let it go, to let Steve Jackson's father come and kill it outright, rather than have to watch its slow and agonizing demise.

What if she simply walked down into the lounge, woke him up and told him to take it, take the whole shebang, take the responsibility off her shoulders? Then, she'd be free. But...free of what? She nearly laughed. Not guilt, that was certain. No, she was in this now and would see it through to the end. Whatever that end might be.

Lissa quickly moved toward Steve. Then she stood gazing at him. His eyes were closed as he breathed in the slow, steady rhythms of deep slumber.

What in the world was he dreaming about, to produce a smile like that?

She had to fight her stupid impulse to smooth that lock of hair off his forehead. Finally winning that battle, she suddenly lost another and picked up a hand-crocheted afghan from the back of a sofa.

Stepping closer, she paused, then stared. There was no longer any doubt whatsoever about the reason for his smile, or what had nudged the magazine off his lap. *Cripes!* She clenched her teeth, not knowing whether she was most annoyed with herself for being impressed, or him for being in that state while he dreamed of...whom?

It sure wasn't ghosts.

She picked up the magazine and dropped it on the table, where it landed with an audible slap. He didn't wake up, though his smile faded and a frown creased his forehead for an instant. Still annoyed with herself, and with him, she spread the afghan over his long frame.

One of his big toes poked through between the imperfectly joined corners of four granny squares, making her smile. He murmured, smiled again, and cuddled the blanket up under his chin.

It took all Lissa's strength to back slowly away from him instead of tucking the covering more securely around his shoulders and fixing it so his toe didn't stick out. How could such a large toe, with a blunt-cut nail and a callus on the side, look so vulnerable? And why did it bring a catch to her throat? She sat down on the sofa next to his chair and watched him sleep.

She was still sitting there, listening to him breathe, aching to touch him, when she heard the distinctive squeak of the swinging doors from the dining room. She leapt to her feet and whirled around. There was Rosa, carrying a tray of rolls and pastries for early risers. Good grief! It was nearly 5:00 a.m.!

In one leap, Lissa started back to her post at the front desk, but she wasn't quick enough.

"What's this?" Rosa whispered, staring at Lissa, hovering between the lounge and the desk, and at Steve Jackson sleeping in a chair. "What's *he* doing down here? I thought you told your dad you wouldn't get involved with him." She gave Lissa an arch grin. "I figured you'd change your mind."

"I didn't change my mind!"

"No, I don't suppose you did." Rosa set her tray on

the reception desk. The mingled scents of cinnamon and yeast filled the lobby. "The mind seldom has anything to do with things like this, does it?"

Lissa was saved having to come up with a suitable reply by the arrival downstairs of George, Mark and Jamie Fredricks.

"Hey there, Lissa!" George boomed. "Have you looked outside yet? Gonna be another great day. Not a rain cloud in sight."

He and his sons each grabbed a couple of rolls, shoved them into the white paper bags the inn provided, and stuffed them into the pockets of their fishing jackets. George turned to Rosa. "Coffee ready yet?" He added apples and oranges to his pockets.

"Comin' right up, boys."

The conversation woke Steve Jackson. Maria and Jacinta Allenda, also dressed for the dawn bite, came in from their cabin near the beach, equally eager to get a few hours' fishing before breakfast.

There was nothing Lissa could do but stand there and stare as Steve sat up and stretched his arms high over his head, arching his back. He yawned, patting his open mouth with the back of one hand and then looked straight at her.

She gazed back at him as he slowly got to his feet, rising like a lithe panther from his lair. He caught the afghan as it slid toward the floor, holding its bright, zigzag pattern bunched in one fist.

She wanted to back away but she was frozen in place.

Something in his expression unleashed a wild, excited rush of blood through her veins. It weakened her knees and made her feel dizzy. Without shifting his gaze from hers, he took a step toward her, tripped over the part of the afghan caught on his toe and turned the fall into a push-up, from which he bounced to his feet.

"There goes another guy, fallin' for Lissa," Jamie Fredricks snickered. "Won't do you any good, Steve," he added as Steve, appearing completely unfazed, grinned. "Lissa's the original unapproachable woman."

"Oh, yeah?" Steve said. He shook the afghan loose from his toe and, still staring at Lissa, carefully folded the blanket twice, then dropped it onto the sofa.

Steve watched a delicate pink flush rise up Lissa's throat to tint her face as he came close to her. "Hey," he said, "thanks for the cover. That was nice of you."

Her lashes fluttered. She shrugged. "You looked...chilly."

She looked warm. "I was dreaming about you," he said, and she suddenly looked a lot more than warm.

As an excuse to touch her, he captured a loose wisp of hair and slipped it behind her ear. Her cheek was satiny, heated, its curve enticing. She shivered.

"Are you sure you aren't hiding some latent mothering instincts deep inside somewhere?" he asked.

She shook her head. "Positive. I don't have a maternal instinct to my name."

Her voice wobbled the faintest bit and a pulse hammered hard in her throat. He touched the tip of his finger to it. He wished it was the tip of his tongue. He wanted to return to last night's fantasy, and this time, make it reality, hear her whispering into his ear, feel the heat of her breath, taste her skin, her lips, her mouth, drag in great gulps of the scent of her hair. He wanted—

"No?" He forced the question out through a suddenly raspy throat. "What kind of instincts do you have, Lissa?"

For a moment, he thought she wouldn't reply as their gazes meshed.

"Strong instincts of self-preservation," she finally said and slipped behind the front desk. Once again she disappeared behind the door in the back wall and closed it firmly behind her.

Aboard her boat, Lissa sat sipping coffee. She should, she knew, go below again, grab a few hours' sleep, then get back to organizing the festival, but it was a glorious morning and she hated to waste it sleeping. The early fishermen had gone out and wouldn't be returning anytime soon, not with the weather so lovely. Steve, she was certain, would be among them.

The sun was shining, the sky was cloudless and the waters of Madrona Cove were shimmering so she remained on deck. She sat back in her hammock chair, her feet propped on the rail, coffee cup propped on one knee and looked out.

"This is Lissa's boat." She heard the marina manager's voice behind her.

"Boss Lady," said a laughing voice that startled Lissa into pushing her toe against the rail, spinning her chair around so fast that most of her coffee slopped out. "Yup, it makes sense."

Merv laughed, too. "One of a kind, she is, our Lissa. Oh!" he added in what some might have taken to be genuine astonishment, "there she is herself."

Steve Jackson standing on the dock in broad daylight was no less attractive than he had been by lamplight. He shaded his eyes with one hand as he peered up at her into the sun.

"Mornin', Liss," Merv went on. "Okay if we come

aboard?'' Without waiting for her reply, he stepped up onto the deck. Steve remained on the float. "You've met Steve Jackson?"

"Yes," she said. "We've met. Planning another day's fishing, Steve?"

"No, I wasn't thinking of going out today."

"Why not?"

He grinned. "Is it compulsory?"

"I...no. Of course not. It's just that's what I thought you'd come for." Too late, she remembered the circumstances under which he'd said those words. "I mean, it's what most of our guests come for."

"I didn't get much sleep last night," he said.

"Really? Looked to me as if you did all right." He'd slept longer than she had, which had been not at all.

"That was just a catnap."

"Problems last night?" Merv asked innocently.

"Not really," Steve said. "I was...restless, I guess. I moved down to the lounge to read, and fell asleep there. Lissa was kind enough to toss a blanket over me."

"Good for her," Merv said, bestowing an approving look on her. "Uh, Liss, I was telling Steve about the renovations we've done to your boat here. I wonder, since you're obviously not too busy, if you wouldn't mind giving him a tour."

As she opened her mouth to refuse, Merv gave her a pointed look. "I promised I'd help Larry with a little job he needs to take care of for the next hour or so."

She suppressed a sigh. *All right, Merv. Message received.*

"I sure hope tonight will be an improvement over last night," Merv said to Steve, with every appearance of sincerity. "The whole Madrona Inn team likes to pull together to make every guest's stay exactly what we all want it to be.''

What could she say? What could she do? She had to show Steve around her boat. Though she'd rather have pitched him in the drink, she conjured up a smile.

"Sure," she said, resigning herself to the inevitable. She'd be a team player if it killed her. "Come aboard. Would you like some coffee? Sugar, milk?"

"Black," he said, his eyes on hers as he strolled beside her on the deck of her old, converted tugboat. "And sweet."

She couldn't force a reply through her throat. He wore faded blue cutoffs with ragged edges. His brown, powerful legs spoke of hours on tennis courts or golf courses or other playboy activities. His blue polo shirt added depth to the color of his eyes and its open neck gave her a tantalizing peek at that golden mat of hair on his chest.

She jerked her gaze away as Merv gave them an insouciant wave and left her alone. Alone with Steve Jackson.

"I—I'll get the coffee," she said, snatching up her own cup. She scuttled below and wasted a good three minutes telling herself she did not need to put on lipstick, did not need to brush blush over her cheeks or powder her nose, did not need to do anything but pour two mugs of coffee and take them outside.

Before she made it back on deck, however, vanity won out.

She even combed her bangs and whipped on a smidgen of mascara, though her dark lashes really didn't need it. But maybe her self-confidence did.

When Lissa returned, Steve had unfolded a canvas chair and set it up near hers. He had both his feet on the starboard rail as he looked out toward the entrance to the Cove. He smiled his thanks as she set his coffee on the deck beside him.

Suddenly, she found she wasn't quite prepared to look at Steve, though she couldn't have said why it was so difficult. All she had to do was be friendly. Keep him entertained. Keep him from returning to his room while Larry did the job that had to be done.

"I was admiring that big house over there on the point," Steve said, breaking a silence that Lissa was beginning to find unbearable. Following the direction of his gaze, she looked at the sprawling, white-shuttered, brown-painted house set in a swath of grass that sloped almost to the water's edge. It had its own wharf and boathouse, and was surrounded by well-established shade and fruit trees. "It looks like a real home."

She eased herself into her swinging chair. "It was," she said. "It was my home when I was a little girl."

He arched his eyebrows. "I thought you lived at the inn."

"My parents split up when I was ten and the house had to be sold. I spent summers here with Dad in the manager's residence on the inn's third floor. The room you first stayed in was mine. The one you have now, was Dad's."

"It must have been fun, living in a hotel." Steve sounded, she thought, wistful.

"Didn't you? You said your father owns resorts. You never lived in any of them?"

He shook his head and changed the subject. Of course, under the circumstances, he wouldn't want to talk about his father's business.

"I like the name of your boat," he said, "*Boss Lady*. It's exactly what I'd have expected—a feminist boat."

"I didn't name her. Maria and Jacinta did. The Allendas? Your table mates?"

He nodded, sipped his coffee, his eyes on her face as if he was waiting for her to go on.

Feeling oddly compelled to do so, she continued. "They bought her, moored her here, had her converted from a tug to a pleasure craft, then realized they really didn't like living aboard and would rather stay in one of the cabins ashore and fish from a runabout. So when I was looking for a place to live, she'd been on the market for several years and I got her for a fraction of her real value."

"You don't mind fishing from a bigger boat?"

"I don't fish." She hadn't intended it to come out so coldly.

He cocked his head. "And you sound disapproving of those who do."

"Sorry. I didn't mean to. It would be sort of hypocritical, wouldn't it, earning my living in a place that caters to sports fishing, if I disapproved."

"But you do," he said. It wasn't a question.

Lissa knew she should deny it, but somehow, the bright sun, the fresh morning and the steady gaze of the man sitting beside her made equivocation more difficult than telling the truth. "To fish for food for yourself or others is okay within reason. It's the greedy desire to catch your limit every day, whether you need the food or not, the insistence on getting the biggest fish, the trophy fish, that bothers me. I absolutely loathe fishing derbies, because they encourage people to toss out the smallest fish from their boat the minute they have a bigger one on board, in order not to go over their daily limit. It's so wasteful, and before long, there won't be any fish left, unless we start conserving them, caring for their habitat, and—''

She broke off and took a hefty swig of her coffee. "Sorry," she said. "That's a hobbyhorse I try to stay off, especially with guests of the inn. But what I'd really like to do is offer them an alternative. With any luck," she said, tapping her toe on the rail, "*Lady* here and I will be able to do that, starting next year. I want to take out parties of photographers, painters, even just sight-seers on day cruises, and maybe overnighters. There has to be an alternative to killing things for entertainment, as badly as we need tourist dollars."

"I agree," he said. "I have a career that takes me into oceans all over the world and I'm probably even more worried about conserving marine life than you are."

Lissa felt her jaw drop. "You have a career?" The words popped out before she could bite them back. She choked, then tried to control it with another gulp of coffee, which only made things worse.

He laughed aloud as he rose and thumped her on the back. "Of course I do," he said over the sound of her coughing. "What did you think I was, a dilettante?"

Since that pretty much covered it, she had to do some fast backpedaling. "I meant a career that takes you *into* the ocean."

"I'm a deep-sea diver," he said as the thumps eased off to gentle pats. "I just finished a contract working with a scientific team studying krill. We were working in Antarctica—the Ross Sea—since early January and just finished up a week ago."

"That must have been, um...cold." *Brilliant, Lissa!*

What a scintillating conversationalist you are! Maybe she could do better if only he'd quit patting her back.

He did, after a last run along her spine with the tips of his fingers. "Yeah, it was cold, all right," he said, then grinned. "And nobody to offer me hot milk, or cover me up at night."

"Surely if you'd gone to one of your father's resorts you'd have been pampered."

"To death," he said wryly. "That's why none of us ever go."

"Us?"

"My older sister and younger brother feel the same way. We're a great disappointment to Dad, in that we didn't follow in his footsteps. My sister's a doctor, my brother's a stockbroker, and I just bum around the world on boats."

That reminder brought her to her feet. And probably to her senses. "Would you...would you like that tour of the boat now?" Anything would be better than sitting there with his hand caressing her spine.

His eager smile did dangerous things to her heart. "Sure," he said. "I'd love to see where you live."

5

STEVE FOLLOWED Lissa down the companionway to the saloon, breathing in the scent of good wood polish mingled with the faint odor of diesel, and something else. He liked the way boats smelled, but this one was special. It had a distinctive aroma, a feminine one that he realized must be due to the fact that a woman lived here, sprayed perfume on herself here, lit scented candles here, used makeup and special bath soap and talcum powder.

No, not just *a* woman. *Lissa.* Lissa, with her thick braid lying on her back where his hand had so recently rested. Lissa, minus her long skirt, dressed now in skimpy shorts that showed her long, slim legs to even better advantage than her jeans had. Bare and tan.

Those were the legs he'd seen hanging through his ceiling, legs whose smooth skin he'd touched. He was almost sure of it.

He wanted, suddenly, and with an intensity that shook him, to run his hands over them from thigh to ankle, to feel the silk of her skin under his palms. One such touch and he'd know. And if he was wrong, which he doubted, it wouldn't matter. He'd gladly forget about the woman with the tattoo, if he could just slide his hands along Lissa Wilkins's perfect legs....

His breathing grew erratic, his throat tightened and he considered a swift retreat, but Lissa turned just then, gesturing toward a door half-behind the companionway they'd descended. He jerked his gaze up, meeting her eyes. It did little to improve his equilibrium.

"There are four double cabins back that way," she said, oblivious to his agony, "and the engine room below."

She showed him into a narrow corridor, opened a door as she passed it and stepped aside so he could enter. The cabin was small but compact, with two single bunks, one over the other, built-in cabinets, a porthole near the ceiling indicating that this cabin was mostly below the waterline, and a skylight that could be opened for air.

"The other three are just the same," she said, and sidled past him on her way back to the saloon. Her scent floated up and made his throat contract again, pulling him along in her wake.

She moved lithely toward the other end of the big main cabin and spun in place, beaming with pride. "Isn't she a beauty?"

"A real beauty," he said, watching sunlit water cast rippling reflections over Lissa's arms and face. Slowly, with the length of the saloon between them, he brought his breathing back under control. Forcing his gaze away from her, he ran his fingers along teak paneling and said, "Excellent workmanship."

"Nice and roomy, too. I don't like cramped quarters," she said. "And despite her size, she handles like a dream, though I doubt I could manage her without the bow-thruster."

The boat *was* beamy, making for a comfortable living area that held two wicker settees, several matching chairs and a masculine looking leather easy chair that seemed oddly out of place. Steve instantly had an image of the chair occupied by the older man Lissa had been with. A coffee table, looking equally heavy and solid, appeared to have been made from an old hatch cover encased in resin. It stood between the two settees. Brass lamps hung from the dark wood ceiling, several were mounted on the walls, and built-in bookcases held a large number of volumes, carefully set behind ledges that would keep them from tumbling out in rough weather. A media center, complete with TV and VCR, was built into cabinets across from the bookcases. All was compact and superbly crafted with fine attention to detail.

"A real home-away-from-home." He'd have liked to sink back into the leather chair and put his feet up on its matching ottoman.

"No," she said with a faint smile as she stroked her fingers over the top of a deeply polished wooden locker, its lid decorated with fine marquetry forming a compass rose. "A real *home,* period. The first one I've ever been able to call my own."

"Yes." He could see that it was her home, and that she loved it.

When was the last time he'd lived any place he could call home? He didn't remember. Wherever he tossed his duffel, he supposed, had become that to him, but seeing what Lissa had done to make this boat all hers showed him a vast lack in his own life.

He ducked to miss a hanging lantern as she led the way forward into the galley area. From there, another companionway led up to the wheelhouse. Sun poured golden light in on the dark-walnut stair treads, glinted off the brass handrail, and warmed the air with dancing dust motes.

He'd liked to have gone up to see the controls, to

ask her about motive power. Hell, he'd like to start the
engines himself, take the boat out, feel its fifty-foot
length responding to seas, currents, winds, answering
to his command. He could almost hear the diesels rumbling through her hull, feel their smooth vibration. A
well-tuned engine in a well-maintained boat was like a
loving woman in the right hands.

He turned to Lissa.

"More coffee?" she asked, lifting the pot from the
top of the stove. Quickly, almost guiltily, he held out
his cup, which she refilled, then topped up her own
before turning toward an open door on the port side.

"This cabin's larger than the aft ones, so I've turned
it into my office for now."

"And where do you sleep?"

"Forward," she said. "Under the wheelhouse."

Her tone, the slight stiffening of her shoulders, told
him with certainty that that was one room she had no
intention of showing him. This one, though, held more
of the type of sketches he'd seen her working on. He
wandered around the small space, looking at each plan
closely. There were more on her desk. As he studied
them, he absently picked up pretzels from a brass bowl
and nibbled on them.

Noticing her amused smile, he said, "Oops. Sorry.
I should have waited to be asked."

"No problem," she said, helping herself to a tangle
of pretzels and nibbling along with him. "That's what
they're there for."

Damn! She had a tantalizing little crystal of salt on
her bottom lip. He had to struggle to keep his eyes off
it. "I'm still interested in renting a booth," he said.
"For my Cinderella search, remember." Though he

was sure enough of his "Cinderella's" identity, he didn't think the search would take very long.

"I'm sorry, but no. They're always spoken for months in advance." If she rented him a booth, it would mean for sure he meant to stay till the festival. Her dad, the committee, and everyone else notwithstanding, she still didn't want that to happen. "Besides, you won't be here."

"Why not?" he said, following her back into the galley. "I have no plans to go anywhere before my vacation's over."

"I...no. Of course not. I, uh, guess I forgot your check-out date." Her laugh sounded phony to her. "People come and go so often, it's hard to remember who will be here when."

He gave her an odd look. "Well, I, for one, will be here...when. So how about you let me have one of the booths that don't pay rent, but give all their proceeds to the fund-raising? I like Madrona Cove, Lissa. I want to contribute in some way."

"Those booths are all spoken for, too," she said, "but there is one I'm sure you'll enjoy if you really want to contribute. You can spend lots of money at it."

He leaned on the wall. "Oh, yeah? What's that?"

"A kissing booth. Run by Caroline Newson."

"Caroline Newson?"

"She's the one who got you kicked out of Chuckles. It's one of the most popular events," she said. "Only two dollars a kiss and all the sales are donated to the community fund."

"I'd rather kiss you," he said.

"Don't be hasty. Caroline has a reputation for killer kisses."

"Don't you?" he said.

She returned to the saloon where there was more space so she wouldn't have to stand so close to him. It was time to end their conversation. Surely Larry had finished setting up the stereo equipment in the attic above Steve's bed. "Not that I'm aware of."

"Maybe you should let someone else judge the quality of your kisses."

"I don't think so," she said, hoping he wouldn't notice the telltale pulse she could feel leaping wildly in her throat.

"If you ran a kissing booth," he told her, stroking a finger down the curve of her cheek, "I'd buy up all your tickets, all your time."

She managed a creditable laugh. "I think you're just scared of Jase. But don't worry. We'll keep him busy all weekend running the jousting tournament."

"I wasn't worried," he said, sliding his hand under her braid. "Are you?"

"I try not to worry," Lissa steadied herself so as to show no reaction to his touch. No reaction? She could only hope she was fooling him. She certainly wasn't fooling herself. Her entire body was one big reaction.

"It gives a girl wrinkles." A little voice in the back of her mind said, *Lissa, stop this. Stop it now. Stop it while you can,* but an even stronger one urged her to discover where it could go.

He stroked her face again, with the pad of a thumb, and it set up a deep, aching longing inside her. "Looks like you've succeeded. I don't see too many wrinkles. How do you prevent worry?"

"By keeping charming rakes at arm's length." She laughed as she spoke, hoping to disguise the tremor in her voice. "And you, Mr. Jackson, are one extremely charming rake, but like all the others I've met, dangerous to my mental health.''

"I am, am I?'' His hands cupped her shoulders. He tugged her closer until their bodies just barely touched. Heat flared through her.

She planted her hands on his chest. "Why are you doing this?'' she asked, appalled at the choked whisper her voice had become.

"Why? Two reasons. One, I want to convince you that not all charming rakes are dangerous.''

"Really?'' She stiffened her arms just a tad—and at the same time, managed to strengthen her voice. "How do you expect to make me to believe that?''

"Well, I could start by kissing you.''

She flexed her fingers against his chest, still unsure just how far she would let this go. "I'd consider that a very, very dangerous move.''

"For you, or for me?''

She pretended to consider the question. How long had it been since she'd flirted like this? She'd once been good at it, once enjoyed it—far too much—and it had brought her all sorts of heartache. It wouldn't again. Somehow, she'd see to that. She was nearly thirty-two. She could handle this. She could handle him. As well as herself and her crazy impulses.

"For both of us, maybe,'' she said.

"Think so?'' His eyes glittered. "You don't strike me as a danger. At least, not an unacceptable one.''

"No? How do I strike you?''

"As a woman I want very much, at this moment, to kiss.''

"Nobody can have everything he wants.''

"Not even charming rakes?''

"Especially not them.''

"How about you? What do you want?"

She lowered her lashes to hide her expression, sure it would be a dead giveaway.

"Come on," he urged, moving his chest against her, slowly, sensuously, so she felt his mat of hair even through his polo shirt and her tank top. She wished she'd put on a bra following her after-work shower. "Tell me what you want, Lissa."

He moved again. No. She had to be honest with herself. She was glad she'd remained braless, glad to feel these kinds of physical sensations again, this kind of wild and heady emotion. The faint motion of the boat in the water made her feel as if the two of them were far away from others, and alone, despite the sounds of voices calling across the marina, the whine of outboards coming and going.

"This?" he asked, sliding his hand down her back and drawing her against him.

She raised her gaze to meet his and answered his question. "No. No, I don't want that."

Liar, liar, pants on fire. Oh, Lord, was that where the phrase had come from? Far more than her pants would be on fire in another couple of seconds.

"I didn't ask what you *don't* want," he said, his voice a husky challenge that echoed the one in his eyes, "but what you *do* want."

"What?" Now, now that it was probably too late, she tried to lighten it up. "And ruin any feminine mystique I might have? A girl's supposed to keep some things secret, isn't she?"

"Not all of them," he said, his voice so low it seemed to vibrate in her bones. "And not all the time. For instance, she shouldn't try to keep secrets from a man who can read the truth in her eyes."

"What truth is that?"

"All your secrets. Your deepest wishes. Desires. Fantasies." He leaned lower, his breath fanning across her lips. "Tell me. *Before* I kiss you and find out for myself how well I read you."

She placed the tips of three fingers over his lips. "You said two reasons. You only gave me one."

He parted his lips, nearly capturing one of her fingers, but she snatched it back before he did more than flick it with the tip of his tongue, but even that small caress heightened the tension between them. It hurt her heart to beat.

"The second reason, Jackson," she reminded him.

"Because you have salt on your lip."

She licked it off, smiled and said, "Sorry, it's gone. I could get you some more pretzels if you're suffering from salt withdrawal."

He grinned. "I'm not suffering from salt withdrawal. I'm suffering from six months in the Antarctic on an all-male ship."

She chuckled, glad the spell had been broken—at least to an extent that made breathing an option again. "Ah, so this isn't personal at all. Anyone would do. You really should wait till the festival and go visit Caroline."

He widened his stance, splayed his fingers open on her lower back, pressing her against him intimately. Her breath stalled as she realized the spell hadn't been broken at all. It had just gained strength.

"Uh-uh," he said. "And it's personal, all right. Very, very personal."

She saw in his eyes, felt in the power of his body, exactly how personal it was. She held herself very still against him, not wanting to tip the balance between teasing and the reality of their mutual, growing desire for each other. A fine tremor shook her as he traced the shape of her eyebrows with his lips. She shivered and wet her lips.

"Well?" he said, lifting his head. "I'm waiting."

"Waiting?" She could have wished for a steadier voice. She could have hoped he wouldn't see the excitement she knew must be brimming in her eyes, the heightened warmth of her cheeks. She might have wished for him not to notice her swift, shallow breathing, and not to feel the quiver running through her like a low-voltage current.

She could have wished for all that, but she didn't. What she wanted was to increase the voltage until they both sizzled.

"Waiting for what?" she whispered.

He dropped his lashes halfway and ran the tip of his finger along her lower lip. "For permission to do what I want. What I've wanted since the first time I saw you."

"You kissed me then, if I remember it right."

"You remember it, but I didn't kiss you right."

She met his gaze, suddenly serious. "You don't strike me as a guy who normally asks permission."

"I'm not," he admitted readily enough. "But maybe these aren't normal circumstances."

They certainly weren't normal for her! "If you're looking for more than a kiss, you better go look elsewhere. It's all I'm offering."

"But you *are* offering?"

"Would it do any good to say I hadn't intended to offer even that?"

He lowered his head and brushed his lips over hers.

"Sure." He grinned, lifting his head. "If you meant it."

"Half an hour ago—ten minutes ago—I would have."

"And now?"

She sighed with more drama than she'd intended, and watched laughter sparkle in his eyes. "I'm afflicted with a terrible thirst for knowledge, a curiosity that knows few bounds. And I've been wondering since that first night what it would be like to kiss you. To be really kissed *by* you. But that's all…"

"If you're sure that's all…"

She slid her hands up over his chest to his shoulders, very conscious of the strength of his muscles, the hardness of his body. He'd be a powerhouse of a lover. The thought made her weak. "That's it, sailor."

"If that's it, that's it. I guess I'll have to take what I can get. Just a kiss."

"Okay, as long as you're sure you won't try to take it any farther. Remember, we're not as alone here as it might seem."

He backed off a bit. "I think I've just been insulted."

"No. Merely warned," she said. "I'm pretty sure you're not accustomed to curtailing your…desires."

"Hah! Spending six months at sea? Of course I am."

"But there's no temptation at sea."

His chuckle was deep, throaty, seductive. "Ah, so you see yourself as a temptation?"

With both thumbs, she stroked the skin in the V of his shirt, then up under his chin, finally bringing her fingers together at his nape. "I won't for much longer if you don't shut up and kiss me."

She knew she'd gotten to him by the roughness of

his voice. "How do you want me to kiss you?" he asked, brushing her lips again. "Like…this?"

He lifted his head as if to gauge her reaction and ran the backs of his fingers from her shoulder to her face. Her lids drifted shut. A raggy breath escaped her. This was more personal than she'd thought it would be, standing in Steve Jackson's arms, toying with him, letting him toy with her. It heightened all her senses, brought her to an intense state of need. It was a whole lot more personal than it ought to be.

He kissed her again, with a little more pressure, the barest flick of his tongue. "Or like that?" he asked.

"Mmm," she murmured noncommittally, without opening her eyes.

"Or maybe this?" he whispered, then covered her lips fully with his.

The sound she made wasn't even close to a word, but he must have recognized assent when he heard it, when he felt it, because she was assenting to that kind of kiss and they both knew it. She was probably assenting to a great deal more, but she wasn't prepared to think about that yet. Enough for now to accept, to feel, to enjoy and to give…

Her head began to spin as Steve parted her lips with his, boldly, surely, masterfully. This man had done lots of kissing. He had honed it to an art. Perfected it beyond any perfection she had ever dreamed of. His lips were hard. They were hot. They were dry.

But his tongue was wet, just as hot, and just as hard.

Nothing could have kept her from accepting its thrust, welcoming it, tilting her head back to offer him more. Joyfully, she caressed his throat, his ears, the back of his neck, then let her eager fingers tunnel into his hair.

Ah, this was like every fantasy come true. His kiss filled her soul even while whetting her body's hunger. He groaned, deepened the kiss, held her tighter, enfolding her. He tangled his hand in her hair, began spreading the strands of her braid apart, massaging her scalp while she tightened her arms around him.

She pressed herself against him, returning his caresses, reveling in his physical response to her, of hers to him, their mutual need building, escalating, whirling out of control.

She wanted him, knew beyond any doubt he wanted her just as much. He spread his legs wider, drawing her in close, one hand on her bottom, right over the tattoo she'd sworn he'd never get a chance to see. The tips of his fingers burned hot against the bare skin of her thigh below the cuff of her shorts.

Now, she knew he was going to see, to touch, a whole lot more of her than a small tattoo. She hooked a leg behind his, running the sole of her foot up his calf, aching for him to lift her off her feet and lay her down on the settee. She rubbed her hands up and down his back as he began to lower her slowly.

"Steve," she murmured. He slid his hands up under her tank top, eased it up, and then covered her breasts with his big, warm hands. She wanted more, much more. She needed his weight, his heat, his mouth where his hand was. She needed his hands everywhere, his kisses everywhere. "Please," she said.

"I want you." His voice rumbled darkly in her ear as his mouth finally took her breast. "So sweet, so hot...Lissa..."

Steve continued to lower her slowly, still kissing her. She settled back willingly, drawing him closer, and—

Wham!

The settee flew backwards, its cushions flying in all directions. Someone's foot knocked over two forgotten cups of cold coffee, splattering it everywhere. And as if all that wasn't horrible enough, Lissa then smashed her elbow into a sharp corner of the coffee table.

"Oh! Oh! Oh!" In pain, she rolled on the floor, moaning, clutching her elbow. "Oooh, that hurts! Damn! But that hurts!" She began rubbing her arm, which was aching like crazy. Tears stung her eyes, and she curled into a ball.

"What? What?" She felt Steve lift her up into a sitting position. She opened her eyes and stared blearily at him. With both his hands still wrapped around her waist, he studied her. "What's wrong? What happened? What did I do?"

"Nothing. The settee slipped. I bashed my elbow." She rubbed it, nursing it tenderly as the pain slowly ebbed.

"We're on the floor." His eyes flicked this way and that. "How did we end up here?"

"We fell."

"This wasn't what I'd planned," Steve said ruefully.

"It wasn't what I'd planned, either," she said.

Steve's hands tightened around her waist and he said, "Here comes trouble, or I miss my guess."

She wiped her eyes with the back of her hand. "Huh?"

Had he brained himself when they missed the settee? "What do you mean?"

He jerked his head sideways. *"Him."*

She followed the direction of his gaze and found her father standing on the last step, staring at them with a look of bewilderment.

"What are you doing here?" she gasped, scrambling

to her feet, sending the upset settee skittering around in a semicircle until one of its legs bashed into Steve, knocking him flat again. Lissa faced her father as he came down the last step and stood erect. "Dammit, couldn't you *knock?*"

"I'm sorry," he said as Steve clambered to his feet, trying to get between Lissa and her father. He took hold of her arm. She wasn't having any of that.

"Let go of me!" She jerked free, tripped on one of the cushions and flopped down onto the only solid chair in the room.

"I'm sorry, too," he said, running a hand through his hair, leaving it all curls and spikes sticking wildly into the air. "It just started as a kiss." It took a moment for Lissa to realize he wasn't apologizing to her, but to her dad.

"Oh, don't be sorry," her father said with an expansive wave of his hand. "Believe me, I know my daughter. She's never been able to resist a charmer. Of course, there isn't a man alive who can resist her, either, so I suppose it evens out. This is just a case of history repeating itself. And about time, too, I might add."

"Dad!" Lissa said.

In the same second, Steve echoed, *"Daughter?"*

"Of course she's my daughter. What did you think?"

"Dammit, Steve, let me handle this," she said. "Dad, what are you doing down here?"

"What did I think?" Steve said as if Lissa hadn't spoken. "I thought when I saw her sitting on your lap in the bar, then saw the two of you leaving with your arms around each other you were...well, you know what I thought."

Her father's face creased with laughter. "I'm flattered," he said as he stepped closer and offered his hand to Steve.

"*I'm* not," Lissa put in, but her dad continued to ignore her, actually reaching around her as if she was nothing more than an annoying intrusion.

"Name's Frank Wilkins," he said.

"Steve Jackson."

"Yeah, I know. I saw you come aboard, thought I'd come down to make your acquaintance. Then I heard a crash and my daughter hollering and yelling, so I figured I'd better just come on in and see who was attacking whom."

"Dad!"

"We had a slight mishap, is all," Steve said.

Lissa watched her father take in the situation. Pure devilment danced in his eyes as he looked around at the trashed saloon, the scattered cushions, the overturned settee. For a moment, his gaze lingered on Lissa's frazzled hair. It was clear he had figured out exactly what had been going on prior to his arrival. "Yeah," he said. "Well, next time, maybe you'd better aim for something more stable." He didn't say *like a bed*, but Lissa knew that was what her father meant.

Obviously, so did Steve. He grinned. "I will."

"Well, I won't," she said, "because there won't be a next time."

"I'd never hurt Lissa," Steve said.

"Yeah, well, she might hurt you, so tread carefully, my son, tread carefully." Her dad laughed, even as she glared fiercely at him.

Steve grinned. "I planned to, but it might already be too late."

Frank nodded. "I know what you mean. That's how

it was with me when it came to her mother. I was a goner in less than thirty seconds.''

"Happens like that sometimes," Steve observed.

"Would you two quit discussing me as if I weren't here?" Lissa put the settee back upright, slammed its cushions in place and sat down on it so hard that she sent it skidding back two feet. Then she crossed her arms and glared at the two men.

"If you don't mind, perhaps you could make each other's acquaintance elsewhere. I have a lot to do today, beginning with getting a few hours' sleep."

Her father sank into the leather chair and swung his feet up onto the ottoman, looking like a man who intended to stay. "Lissa works too hard," he said, waving Steve to another chair. Instead, Steve sat down on the other end of the settee, which put him much too close to her. She pulled her arms in tight around her waist.

"So I gather," Steve said. "We've, uh, been discussing Madrona Madness."

"Madness." Lissa muttered. "There should have been more discussion and less madness."

"What was that?" her father asked.

"Never mind."

Laughing, Steve leaned forward, hands linked loosely between his knees, the picture of a man at ease, and spoke to her father. "I understand you're planning an archery contest for the festival. Sounds like fun. I used to be a pretty good archer when I was in college. Maybe I could coach some of the kids."

Frank beamed. "Sure, why not?"

"Because he's not going to *be* here, Dad!"

Steve shot her a startled look.

"Lissa's been researching an authentic Sherwood

Forest costume for me," Frank said. "I figure I'm a bit long in the tooth and round in the gut for Robin Hood, so maybe I'll be Friar Tuck instead." He grinned and ran a hand over his crisp hair. "Might have to shave this, to get the right tonsure. What do you think?"

"Nah, I doubt it, though I'm no expert, but if you could use a little help with the research, my mother's a collector and trader in antiques, both furniture and clothing. She wouldn't have anything going back to medieval days, of course, but probably knows Web sites where we could get information."

"Well, now, that's mighty kind of you, son. We never turn down a volunteer."

"Dad..."

"What would you like me to do?" Steve asked. "I mean, besides coaching the kids."

"Well, let's see now. I think you'd make a great Robin Hood. Can you see yourself in green tights and a—?"

"No," Lissa said, getting to her feet. "No, he cannot. Dad, Steve is a guest. If he's still here when the festival's on, he should be allowed simply to enjoy it, not be put to work."

"Melissa—" her father said as if she were four years old "—don't interrupt, dear." Then, with scarcely a change in tone, he went on, "Well, what do you think? You interested?"

"I'm interested all right."

"Well, then, fine," she said. "Why don't the two of you sit here and discuss your green tights? I, for one, am going to get some rest before I tackle the stuff I have to accomplish today. Dad, lock the door when you and Steve leave, please."

Her father grinned, not moving. "In other words, get out, get out now, and take my boyfriend with you?"

Through clenched teeth, Lissa said, "He is not my boyfriend. I don't have *boyfriends* anymore, Dad. I'm not a teenager. I don't *want* boyfriends anymore. I simply want to be left alone to do my job until such time as I'm free to do what I really want." She looked pointedly at her father. "I think you get my drift?"

She thought her exit was dignified and ladylike— until she skidded on a magazine that had been knocked to the floor and did the splits between the saloon and the galley.

To their credit, neither man laughed. Steve helped her to her feet, smiled directly into her eyes and said, "See you later."

"Not if I see you first," she muttered, and then realized she had sounded all of twelve years old.

It was too late to take it back, so she tried to exit with the few shreds of dignity she had left. This had not been her finest hour.

6

STEVE USED his room key to open the side door of the inn and stepped silently inside. It was nearly three o'clock in the morning and everyone was sleeping. He'd spent the evening aboard a sailboat moored at the marina, visiting with a congenial couple he'd met at the inn. They were on the last leg of a round-the-world cruise, and had many fine tales to tell. Each time he'd made to leave, they'd urged him to stay and opened another bottle of wine.

The last couple of hours, he'd declined the wine, but continued to enjoy the stories. Even after leaving them, though, he hadn't felt ready for bed, so he went for a walk, enjoying the whisper of the breeze in the branches of the madrona tree and the starry beauty of the night sky. He knew he should be tired considering the hour, to say nothing of a day spent giving kids pointers on archery, helping restring homemade bows and helping to weight homemade arrows, but he wasn't.

He felt as if he'd never want to sleep again. What he wanted to do was relive those crazy moments he'd spent with Lissa. Maybe that was why he'd kept himself so busy all day and half the night, to try to keep thoughts of her, memories, at bay.

But, when he was alone, they came crowding in.

He eased the door shut, making sure it was securely

locked. Then, as he turned, he saw the glow of a lamp in the lounge. It cast a circle of light over Lissa's dark hair, sending shafts of copper, topaz and mahogany through it. She held a book on her lap, but gazed up at him. She rose to her feet and met him as he came down the last step into the lounge.

Tonight, her skirt was shorter, just above her knees, and she wore a sleeveless blouse with it. Her feet were bare, her braid slightly frayed, but her eyes glowed with a luminosity that spoke of things he wanted to hear. Her scent rose to him, tightening his throat. He'd avoided her since that morning's episode aboard her boat, knowing they both needed space. But the time for that was over.

"Hi." She sounded as if she was experiencing the same kind of difficulty he was in getting oxygen to her lungs. Maybe she, too, had done some hard thinking.

"Busy?"

She shook her head.

"Shouldn't you be sleeping?" If she wanted to escape, he wanted to give her the opportunity. Wanted to? No! But he knew he should. What he wanted was to rush her, to rush with her into a hot love affair—and maybe more.

"I did," she said. "For a while."

He took a step closer. "And then?"

He watched her swallow. "And then I...woke up. You're out late."

He told her where he'd been. "After I left them, I went for a walk and...thought."

"Oh."

"I think we need to talk," he said.

For a long moment, she continued to gaze at him. He gazed back, noting the play of emotions on her lovely, expressive face. Holding out his hand, he said, "Come with me?"

Her eyes widened for a second. "Where?"

"Back to where you were sitting, Lissa. Where we can talk in comfort."

Her relief was almost palpable. What, he wondered, would she have said if he had invited her up to his room? He almost wished he had. He considered doing it now, but she squared her shoulders, tilted her chin up and became the Lissa he'd first met, sure of herself, secure in her skin, and with a flicker of humor lurking in her eyes.

"Sure," she said. "Would you like something to drink?"

"I thought the bar was closed."

She glanced over her shoulder as she glided away from him, and toward the bar. "I think I could probably scare up a soft drink or juice. Or get some coffee from the kitchen."

He kept close enough behind her to breathe in the scent of her. "No hot milk?"

She grinned as he leaned on the bar while she went behind it. "Only if you insist."

He wanted to kiss her laughing mouth so badly he could taste it. "I'll have a Coke."

She took a step back. "You will not! I thought you said you wanted to talk, Jackson."

He blinked in bewilderment. "Can't we talk and drink Coke at the same time?"

"You didn't say anything about Coke. You said you'd have a *kiss*."

"I did not!" He played back his words. He was sure of what he'd said. Or was he? Could his unruly imagination have overpowered his mouth? "It must have been your imagination. Maybe you heard what you wanted to hear.''

She slapped an icy can into his hand as she emerged from behind the bar with a bottle of orange juice for herself.

"I heard what you said. If anyone made a Freudian slip, it was you, not me. But let's get one thing straight before we so much as sit down. It's a drink and talk, or bed.''

He laughed outright at her wide, horrified eyes, the hand she clapped over her mouth as she realized what she'd said. "Talk about Freudian slips!" he said. "But if those are my options, I'll take bed. Anytime. With you.''

"That's enough,'' she said, but ruined her attempt at severity with a splutter of laughter. "Remember what happened before.''

"I'll never forget,'' he said, sobering. "Will you?''

"Of course I will.'' She switched on a reading lamp as she crossed behind the wingback chair where she'd once found him sleeping. "It was just a kiss, Steve, and it's not going to be repeated.''

"Was it?'' he asked, catching her in his arms. "Then if it was just a kiss, what harm would there be in repeating it? Didn't you enjoy it?''

She gently moved out of his arms and sat down on the sofa. "There wouldn't be much point in lying about that, would there? I enjoyed it. But that doesn't mean I intend for it to happen again.'' She cranked the top off her orange juice and shoved a straw into the bottle.

Steve sat down abruptly beside her as her lips pursed around the straw. "So you get to make all the rules, all the decisions?'' Even to him, his voice sounded strangled. Jeez! Did she have any idea what she was doing to him?

"Better me than you," she said, setting her juice on the coffee table.

He rolled the cold can of pop across his forehead. "Why?"

"Because I think I'm the more sensible of the two of us." She smiled. "And I didn't just spend six months in the Antarctic."

He set his can down. "Your dad told me you haven't had a date since you came back here over two years ago."

"You discussed me with my dad?" she said as she shot to her feet.

"He discussed. I listened."

Anger flared in her eyes. "He had no right. *You* had no right. My life is—"

"Your business," he interrupted, standing up and clasping her elbows in both hands. "And don't worry. After making that comment, he apparently realized it, and clammed up. Of course, that might have had something to do with the arrival of about three hundred kids between the ages of eight and seventeen, each one equipped with a bow and quiver of arrows."

She laughed, her tension easing. "There aren't three hundred kids in Madrona Cove. There aren't three hundred inhabitants."

"Well, there might have been thirty," he said. "I tend to exaggerate a bit."

He slid his hands from her elbows to her shoulders. "But I didn't exaggerate what your kiss did to me today, Lissa. And that's what I want to talk about."

She was silent for a long moment. "I'm not sure discussing something like that is of any benefit. We kissed. It got a little out of hand. That was just...chemistry."

"Some people say that chemistry makes the world go 'round."

"That's not the way I've heard the quote."

He nodded. "I know. So what are we going to do about it?"

"Nothing," she said. "Nothing at all."

"Oh, I don't think that's possible," he said. "It's not something we can really ignore."

"But we don't know each other well enough."

"We could take care of that. You get time off, don't you? Let's go out together, get to know each other."

"You mean...date?"

Her response amused him. "I'm sure, even if you haven't done it much these past couple of years, it's not an entirely new concept for a woman who's been engaged six times."

"No, but..."

"But what?"

"I—I don't know, really. I guess it's something to do with Madrona Cove, the whole of Quadra Island in fact, being such a small community. No one has any privacy here. Everyone I know, which means everyone here, would be stopping by to make sure you were treating me right, and probably explain that they had a right to check on me because they'd changed my diapers or something equally embarrassing."

"You get days off, don't you? How about we get away from this island, go someplace where no one knows you, act like a normal couple getting to know each other, and—"

She shook her head, deflating his smile. "I'm sorry. I can't."

"Why?"

"I won't be here. When I come off duty tomorrow—I mean, this—morning, I'm going to visit my mother in Tofino."

"I'd like to see the west coast of Vancouver Island," he said.

"Steve..." While he saw temptation, maybe even consideration of the idea in her eyes, he heard regret in her voice. Unwilling to give up, he slid his hand around her and gently stroked the nape of her neck. Her skin was warm and soft and faintly moist.

"Don't say no," he said.

"I thought I just had."

"Not very convincingly. Would it be such a shock to your mother if you arrived with a man in tow?"

She broke into laughter and relaxed, leaning back against his hand. "My mother's on her fourth husband. She considers me a total failure in the man-catching department."

"Wouldn't you like to prove her wrong?"

She looked horrified. "Not if it meant actually *catching* one."

A strange sensation came over him, as if something inside had grown heavy and started sinking, and it triggered unexpected anger. "Why? What's so wrong with men that you wouldn't want to catch one?"

"Hey!" She pulled away. "That wasn't meant as a slur. It's just the way I am. I don't see men as prey and have utterly no desire to 'bag' one, as if he were a trophy. I'd have thought you—any man—would find that a relief."

"Hey, I'm just asking you out on a date," he said.

"I realize you only asked me for a date," she said. "But I have a strange quirk. When I get close to a man, there's a part of me that always wants to get closer.''

He laughed, almost relieved, and deliberately misunderstood as he sank down beside her. "When I'm close to you, honey, there's a part of *me* that wants to get closer, too."

Her eyes flared with anger again. "That's not what I'm talking about! But 'dates' are how relationships usually start. One date at a time. And I don't want a relationship. I mean, maybe I do, but I don't like the inevitable outcome."

"Which is?"

"I get hurt," she said, her voice sounding surprisingly small and defenseless. Her words came slowly now, almost as if she were talking to herself. "I find myself looking for...intimacy, I suppose I'd have to call it, and suffering disappointment when I don't find it. Then the relationship ends. I guess I've always been attracted to the wrong kind of man. I don't want it to happen again."

Again, he felt himself bristling. Nothing could contain it. He wanted to take on the men who had done this to her. He wanted to prove that he wasn't necessarily the wrong kind of man. He wanted to hold her close again, kiss her until she quivered the way she had this morning. Before he could stop himself, he'd pulled her into his arms.

He dipped his head and brushed a brief kiss over her mouth. She stared at him, completely still but for a faint fluttering of her bottom lip. A soft sigh trembled out of her. "Steve..."

"You see what I'm talking about?"

"I always did," she said. "That's why I said it was an experiment we shouldn't repeat."

He stroked a thumb over the curve of her cheek. "But it seems we are."

"Are we?"

"Aren't we?"

She smiled. "I'm not sure."

"I wish you wouldn't smile at me like that," he said.

"Like what?"

"I can't describe it," he said. "It's just the way you smile and it does something to me."

"I'll try not to," she said solemnly, then smiled.

Steve groaned. The need to touch her skin overcame him and he stroked his palm down her bare arm, then back up to her shoulder where he slid a finger under her sleeveless blouse. When he felt a tremor course through her, he took her mouth again.

This kiss was not brief, nor was it casual. It was tender and sweet and enormously appealing, and that disturbed her deeply. If he'd been aggressive, demanding, even masterful, she might have been able to withstand the assault on her senses, but he was giving, not taking, and she accepted his gift.

All the words she'd once believed in—destiny, fate, kismet, ran through her mind. But none of those words could possibly be real. Only, his kiss felt real. His hand, sliding through the plaits of her braid, loosening it, felt real. His mouth, soft on hers, moving over her cheek, down her throat, up to her ear, felt real.

It had to be a dream, but it wasn't—it was real.

Still she wished it wasn't really happening to her. She didn't believe in happy endings anymore, yet what was happening between them seemed to lead in that direction.

They'd met, they'd been attracted, and now here she was, locked in his arms for the second time in twenty-four hours and she wanted more of the gifts he offered.

"Steve," she murmured, her palm cradling his cheek. "We shouldn't... I think..."

"I can't think," he said. "I don't want to think. I want to feel. Feel this with me, Lissa."

She moaned and opened her mouth to him, then turned to make it easier for him to unfasten the buttons down the front of her blouse. His kiss was deep, thrilling, destroying whatever vestiges of good sense she had left. It was a kiss she wanted never to end, but it did.

Even as she cried out in protest, his breath, hot and moist, spread over the tops of her breasts. She gasped, and he answered her unspoken plea, suckling a nipple through the satin of her bra. It wasn't enough, not nearly enough, for either of them. He slid his hand around her back, fumbling for the clasp.

"Here," she said, pressing the button that released the garment in the front. She put one hand under a breast, lifting it, offering it to him. For a moment, he didn't touch it, but gazed at her, his eyes darkly luminous, glowing with passion, then he shut them as he bent and closed his mouth over her.

She raked her nails down his back, around to his chest, slid her hands up under his sweatshirt and over his ribs. He quivered at her touch, and moved to her other breast, bending her back over his arm. Her fingers found one of his hard little nubs in the hair of his chest, teased it, tugged on it, drawing forth a long, low growl of pleasure.

Her heart felt as if it would burst. Her mind swirled with sensation. Her entire body pulsed with a need that only he could fill. He ran a hand from her knee to her hip, under her skirt, his palm scraping deliciously against her skin.

She made a sound. It might have been a word. Whatever it was, she knew he'd understood it because he met the need flaring through her. He cupped her sex with his hand, sliding his fingers over the fabric of her underwear, then up, across her belly. His hand slipped under the elastic, slid through her hair, two fingers parting her folds. And she flew apart.

She squeezed her eyes tightly shut, buried her face against Steve's chest and wept, so stirred was she by the force of her release.

"No, no," she heard him saying. "Don't...please don't."

"I didn't mean... I didn't want... That wasn't supposed..."

"Lissa." He lifted her face, his pale and strained, but oddly triumphant, as if he had fought to reach a high mountain peak and achieved his goal. "I didn't mean for it to happen, either. But I did want it to. You just gave me the most valued gift a woman can ever give a man."

She closed her eyes, felt his lips sipping at the tears that continued to pour forth. She, who hadn't cried for years, brought to this by the touch of a man's hand. It was terrible. She was so ashamed, so embarrassed, she wished she could disappear.

"I gave you nothing," she choked.

His voice was a low rumble against her ear as he murmured, "You gave me your trust."

She could have denied it. Should have denied it. She didn't trust him. She trusted no man. What was more, she trusted herself even less. Especially after this.

"Lissa..." She resisted the pressure of his hand under her chin. "Come on. Look at me."

She shook her head. "I want you to go away."

"That's not going to happen. I'm in this for the—"

For the what, she wasn't to learn, because at that moment, the dining-room doors squeaked open. Rosa came through them, let out a squawk that could have been heard clear across the island, and then simply stared as Steve and Lissa untangled their bodies from each other and stood.

With the back of one hand over her mouth, Lissa stared back at Rosa, whose tray of pastries slowly tilted until cinnamon rolls bounced around her feet, raspberry Danishes splatted face-first onto the carpet, and bran muffins rolled down the stairs into the lounge.

Finally the tray itself clanged to the floor. "Melissa Ann Wilkins, I am *shocked!* Your father said 'make nice,' not 'make love'!" Then she whirled around, bashed the doors open with one thrust of her arm and marched back through them, leaving the scent of cinnamon heavy in the air.

Cinnamon and masculine cologne and sex...

"What did she mean, 'make nice'?"

Lissa stared at Steve, unable to force so much as a single word out of her mouth. She spun away from him, bolted toward the inner office and locked the door.

After escaping out the back way in a frenzied daze, she made her way to her boat. There she threw a few things into a tote bag, called Pete, the manager, and woke him with the news that she'd left the desk unattended.

She hung up on his wheezing complaints, his threats, his accusations of laziness, locked the door of her boat and nearly flew up the ramp to the parking lot. She backed her car out in a spray of gravel that spattered against a red Dumpster, and headed for the road. She'd be early for the first ferry, but she didn't care.

What, oh what, had she allowed to happen to her? If she could, she'd find a way never to return to Madrona Cove. Maybe, with any kind of luck, Rosa would keep her mouth shut, but she doubted it. Rosa would just have to tell someone, in confidence of course, and that person would tell the next, and the next, and before she knew it, everyone in the Cove would be fully aware that Lissa Wilkins had been caught in a compromising position on a couch in the lounge of the Madrona Inn.

With a guest!

A guest who should have been in his room, being kept awake by horrifying sounds, disturbed by weird events, but who had been with her.

If Rosa hadn't interrupted them, she'd likely still be in a state of unreality, where she could pretend Steve Jackson was just a man she liked, a man she desired. A man she could very, very easily fall for.

If she hadn't already done so.

Which meant she hadn't changed a bit, not deep inside where it mattered. She was still a total pushover for any charming man.

She drove aboard the ferry with one eye on her rearview mirror, half convinced Steve was going to come after her and demand an explanation of Rosa's words. She knew she was running away. Well, it wasn't the first time she'd done that. But this time, more than any other time in her life, what she wished she could run from permanently was the disastrous state of her own emotions. She'd met the man a week ago Friday, for heaven's sake! What was she thinking of, falling in love with him by Sunday, just over a week later?

She argued that point with herself all the way across to Campbell River on the ferry, telling herself she was *not* in love. She might be in lust, but she was absolutely, positively, definitely not in love with Steve Jackson.

She repeated it like an incantation as she drove south down the Island Highway, then cut west at Parksville. She didn't even stop at Coombs, as she usually did, to buy fresh fruit from the market with grass and goats on the roof, but kept on driving.

When she finally lifted her cramped, exhausted body from her car and rang her mother's doorbell, she was sure she'd convinced herself.

But the minute she saw her mother she burst into tears. "I'm not in love with him, Mom! Honest I'm not!"

Her mother gathered her close. "Of course you're not, angel. What a ridiculous notion. Who is he, anyway? Come on. Tell me all about him."

SUNDAY NIGHT, Steve lay on his bed with his hands stacked behind his head, staring at faint flickers of light on the dark ceiling, thinking about Lissa. Then the noises started, soft, faint, low, but growing gradually louder. Sobbing, moaning, wailing. His hair stood on end.

Something white and filmy fluttered off to his left.

Turning on the light, he saw the white lace curtains blowing in the light breeze. The air smelled clean and washed, like salt and low tide, evergreens and moss.

He opened the front window wide, pushed back the fluttering curtains, and breathed deeply as he listened to the gentle lap, lap, lap of waves on the shore below and gazed up at the stars shining brightly in the inky sky.

Then, it returned, softly, the sound of sobbing followed by a squeak. His every instinct told him to continue gazing out the window, that if he didn't turn, didn't see, no dresser drawer would have opened. He turned, in time to see the top left one closing.

The sobbing ceased, and the silence was almost as bad.

Moments later he flinched at the sound of a maniacal laugh, high-pitched, hysterical, and definitely coming from overhead. When it faded, the quiet sobbing started again, then tapered off once more. Again he heard only the soothing sounds of the ocean on the shore.

Steve was not soothed. Maybe ghosts sobbed, maybe they opened and closed drawers, maybe they moved clothing inside closets with firmly shut doors. Maybe they laughed, loud and witchlike, then sobbed again, faint and far away. Maybe they even made thumping noises overhead.

But not damned likely.

And for sure they didn't fall through ceilings.

One way or another, he meant to find out what the hell was going on and who was trying to scare him out of the Madrona Inn.

He did a quick search of the corridor, but could find no access to the attic, unless it was behind the locked door near the head of the stairs. The only other locked door led to his old room.

But wait a minute…his old room. Now there was a possibility. He entered the bathroom, tried the door to the adjoining quarters and stepped through it.

He turned on the light. There was nothing there. The bed had been stripped and the trunk stood in a corner, but little else had been done to clean up the mess. He stood under the hole and listened again, scarcely breathing. Not a sound came from the attic. But sounds *had* come from there.

Frowning, he returned to his room, rummaged in an outer pocket of his duffel until he found a flashlight, then moved back through the bathroom to the other room.

It should have been an easy matter to drag the high-boy close to the bed, but it resisted his tugging, then finally gave way with snapping sounds and tiny *sproings* that sounded like springs or wires breaking. He looked behind it.

Well, well, and well again!

At least now he knew how the drawers had been opening and closing seemingly without aid. Springs and wires had indeed broken loose, springs and wires that emerged from neatly drilled holes in the wall.

What lay behind the wall where the dresser had stood? He pictured the layout in his mind. Right. That storage cupboard in the hallway. He'd check that out later. Now, though, he opened the clothes closet in this room, knowing it backed onto the one next door, and sure enough, there was an almost invisible slit behind and below the bar. He wouldn't have seen it if he hadn't left his closet open and the bedside light on. On the floor lay a slender but strong piece of metal, just long enough to reach through the crack and reposition the clothing in his closet.

"Yup!" he said. "Things are getting very, very interesting."

Now, let's see about the sobbing and moaning and laughing of the "ghost."

7

AFTER FINALLY managing to shunt the dresser aside, Steve climbed on top of it and from there poked his head and shoulders through the hole, though it was a tight wiggle to get his arms and hands up, even one at a time. Impatiently, he broke away more plaster, making sure it fell on the bed. He wanted no more complaints from the downstairs guest.

Shining the flashlight around, he saw old furniture stored a few yards away in the highest part of the attic; a bentwood rocking chair his mother would probably pay big bucks for, as well as an armoire for which she might even kill.

A veritable treasure trove. He wished he could investigate, but he had no time for that now.

Slowly, he sent the beam of light gliding this way and that until he'd swept the entire area with it. Besides a heavy coating of cobwebs, there was a draped black electrical cable coming out of a dangling wire between two roof trusses and disappearing off into the dimmer recesses of the attic. There were desks, tables, more chairs, old lamps and sundry unidentifiable items covered with dusty sheets.

There were also footprints in the dust. No ghosts he'd ever heard of left footprints.

He set the flashlight down, wrapped his hands over two floor joists and hauled himself through the hole.

Halfway up, he realized why his mystery woman had needed a boost. The sloping roof got in his way, forcing him to crawl, scraping his belly on the rough joists.

Then, he was up, sitting on a rafter, his upper body bent sideways to accommodate the slope of the roof. With difficulty, he got his feet under him and crouched, duckwalking toward the dangling electrical cord, then following it to its end. There, surprise, surprise, he found a power bar into which were plugged two timers. One, set for 1:30, had already ticked on by. The other, set for 3:30, was slowly clicking. Attached to those timers were two separate tape players.

He manually advanced the 3:30 timer. With a click and a whir, a tape kicked into action, filling the attic and presumably the room below—his room—with the sounds of moaning, sobbing and sighing. There was silence for several minutes, then a faint and ghostly laugh began, rising and falling, before fading away to nothing. Finally there was a sobbing wail that gradually died down.

Carefully, he erased both tapes, then set the clocks back to the correct times. Still crouching, he waddled back to where he could stand erect. At one end of the floored area, footprints in the dust led to a narrow flight of stairs. He descended, reaching a landing and a door. It opened without a sound and he found himself in an alcove off a living area, furnished with more of those antiques his mother would covet.

The view, looking out over the marina, was the same as the one from his bedroom, so the two rooms must be right next to each other, he concluded.

Farther into the room, he found what he was looking for. No attempt had been made to hide the ingenious, complicated setup of springs, wires and more timers, with neat little holes drilled through the wall, holes he knew accessed the back of the dresser in his new room.

He couldn't help laughing. It was, he had to admit, very well done. Now he knew how and why his dresser drawers could open apparently on their own. Leaving the equipment as he found it, he explored further, finding a kitchenette, a small dining room and a door that accessed the corridor near the head of the stairs.

Okay, so someone had gone to a lot of trouble to persuade him there was a ghost in the Madrona Inn. But why? Maybe this was done to every guest who inhabited the top floor? Somehow, though, he didn't think so. Nope. The little piles of sawdust from the drill smelled fresh, and probably had been created within the last few days. This prank was aimed directly at him, and he meant to get to the bottom of it.

Mounting the narrow stairs again, he tiptoed across the attic to the hole and slithered back through. He replaced the dresser, entered the bathroom and locked the door from the inside.

He lay on his bed, thinking. What the hell was it all about? Why *his* room? *Why him?*

Because someone had it in for him? And not just one person. Too many had made a point of telling him about the "ghost." It was as if there was a conspiracy against him, something personal. Did it tie in with Rosa's inexplicable remark about making nice, not making love? How could it? How could scaring a guest qualify as making nice? It couldn't, so there could be no connection there. Yet, Lissa's stricken face had suggested there was.

Dammit, it didn't make any sense. But, then, he decided, turning out the light and trying to compose himself for some much-needed sleep, nor did it make sense to worry about it. Nothing in the Madrona Inn was going to hurt him. One thing he'd learned aboard ship was the best retaliation for a practical joke was never to let on you'd been trapped by it, or even become aware of it. The most fun was yet to come, and the last laugh would be his. He lay back and chuckled about the frustration the perpetrators would suffer when he spent every night happily in this room, always denying, when asked, that anything disturbing had happened.

Nobody pushed Steve Jackson around.

He laughed again. Well, except maybe a logger with a protective attitude toward his lady, and that was something Steve could easily relate to. If the shoe had been on the other foot, would he have acted any differently?

He didn't think so.

And speaking of shoes...

RETURNING FROM TOFINA, Lissa blinked in astonishment when she saw the first sign as she drove through Campbell River. Maybe she hadn't read it right. It was raining, the windshield was smeary and she was tired from two days nonstop talking and shopping with her mother, who thought both were excellent ways to entertain her daughter and take her mind off her troubles. But she saw the next sign as she waited for a light to change. It, she certainly read right.

MADRONA MADNESS
A FESTIVAL TO REMEMBER
JULY 16 & 17
MADRONA COVE, QUADRA ISLAND

She saw three more signs along the highway before she reached the ferry. *What the heck?* Where had they come from? Vivid, eye-catching and professionally prepared, they were well beyond the budget the committee had set for advertising. The last one, right at the ferry terminal, read:

MADRONA MADNESS
FEATURING THE CINDERELLA SEARCH!
IF THE SHOE FITS...
YOU COULD BE
THE GRAND PRIZEWINNER!
TICKETS $2.00 EACH OR 3 FOR $5.00

Oh, Lord! He was going to do it! Who the hell had given him a booth?

A FISHPOND WITH A DIFFERENCE
BAIT YOUR HOOK FOR PRINCE CHARMING
WIN BIG, WIN OFTEN
EVERY TICKET WINS
EACH TICKET BUYS THREE TRIES

A fishpond? She envisioned women from far and wide lining up to buy their tickets to catch a shoe. Unknown to the poor suckers, time after time after time, he'd try the same shoe on each woman, hoping like mad to finally find the one it fit and solve the puzzle of who had fallen through his ceiling.

It was not only a crazy scheme, it was doomed to failure. Rosa would never buy a ticket, never try on that sandal, not even to get her precious Birkenstock back.

But...what if someone else had exactly the same size foot as Rosa? One of the women visitors, for instance?

Someone from one of the Vancouver Island towns, or Heriot Bay or Quathiaski Cove? Even a tourist off a boat at the marina?

He wouldn't care whose foot he had in his hands, whose foot fit that sandal. He was simply looking for someone to offer that wonderful "grand prize" to. She hadn't forgotten their conversation the first night they'd met. She'd considered the suggestion a joke, but clearly, he had not, and what he was going to offer was—himself!

THE CINDERELLA SEARCH IS ON!
PRIZES GALORE

Prizes? Plural? Suddenly it struck her. He had one shoe. How were there going to be multiple winners? What did he mean, "every ticket wins" and "three tries per ticket"? What was he going to do, share himself around? The closer she got to Madrona Cove, the thicker the signs became, and the deeper her irritation.

NOW'S YOUR CHANCE
TO PLAY CINDERELLA
COME AND MEET
THE TRUE PRINCE CHARMING
ALL PROCEEDS TO THE MADRONA COVE
COMMUNITY FUND

Hah! The True Prince Charming, indeed! Was there no end to the man's ego? She tried to forget how easily he had charmed her, how she had fallen like a ripe plum off the tree, right into his hands. Her two-day absence and her mother's wise advice had fortunately given Lissa a better perspective on the whole issue. She remembered now why she had sworn to avoid Steve Jackson in the first place. He was a charmer, and charmers were bad news. Even her mother agreed with that.

"Steer clear of the man," she'd counseled. "Keep out of his reach. You'll be better off without him. He's obviously looking for a vacation fling. Let him have it with someone else. How about your friend Ginny? Seems to me she's constantly on the prowl and would be exactly his type."

At that, she'd informed her mother tartly that if anyone deserved a vacation fling, it was she, herself. "So, what's your problem?" her mother had asked. "Enjoy it, then."

What kind of a mother would say that to her daughter? She'd clamped her mouth shut on the question. *Whatever.* It didn't matter to her. She'd been away two days, and here he was with his stupid Cinderella search well under way, which just proved how fickle he was.

As she stepped off the dock onto her boat, she found a brochure slipped into the crack of her doorjamb, detailing his fishpond plan pretty much as she'd already figured it out. She stood there in the thickening, foggy drizzle, reading it.

Every lady who tried on a shoe that didn't fit also got a consolation prize—a kiss from him.

What? Completely outraged, she crumpled the brochure and flung it toward the rain-pocked water. It bounced off the rail and rolled back to her along the deck. She stared down at it, then stomped on it.

Not only was he running a fishpond with shoes as the catch, but a kissing booth as well? Who the hell did he think he was? And what made him think women would line up to try on his shoes and accept his kisses? Unless those prizes were pretty damned spectacular.

She grabbed up the ball of paper, smoothed it out as best she could and read on with growing dismay. First prize was two weeks at Happy Valley Hot Springs, which she knew to be one of his father's vacation resorts, "with the escort of the winner's choice."

Naturally, he'd expect to be that escort.

Second prize was one week at the same destination, same terms, and third prize, a weekend.

The other prizes dropped by increments of fifty dollars from five hundred in cash to fifty, and there were four of those fifty-dollar prizes.

Oh, for sure he'd have no trouble at all selling tickets with prizes like that.

She wadded up the damp brochure and clenched it in her fist before flinging it again. This time it cleared the rail and bobbed in the water, drifting slowly away with the outgoing tide. He was exactly as she'd first pegged him, a philandering charmer who couldn't be trusted not to dole out his kisses indiscriminately.

The entire thing was such an offensive idea! *Women* ran kissing booths. Men did *not*. He was as good as selling himself to the women who bought tickets. Women, she knew perfectly well, would be lining up for days to get as many chances as they could afford. Because of the prizes, of course, not the kisses. But still, he'd be happily dispensing those. *Disgusting!*

Well, she, for one, wasn't going to play his game or buy even *one* of his tickets.

INSIDE THE CABIN, the light on her answering machine was blinking frantically. The first two calls were from Steve. She closed her eyes and let his warm voice wash over her. "Lissa, I know you're upset. I wish you'd stayed and talked to me before you ran off like that. We'll sort it out when you get back. Nothing's going to happen unless you want it to happen. That's a promise. You can trust me. Okay?"

"No," she said. "It is not okay. Nothing's okay. And there is nothing to sort out." Especially considering the person she couldn't trust was herself, not Steve.

Probably, if she'd realized the next call was from him, too, she'd have rewound the tape right then, erasing everything on it without listening. But she didn't know, and the minute his voice came drifting up around her, it was as if she were caught in some kind of immobilizing web. "I talked to your dad about putting in a booth. He and the rest of the committee agreed, the more the merrier, and since he got Larry Cranshaw to play Robin Hood to his Friar Tuck, I figure I can make more money for the fund with my Cinderella booth. What do you think? Isn't it a great idea? How do you like the signs?"

"Oh, sure," she said. "A great idea. I love the signs." She ran both hands through her hair, shoving off the scrunchie that held it back. "I'm going to go and rip them out, one by one, break them into kindling and pitch them into the nearest incinerator!"

The rest of the calls were from her father and friends, filled with chuckling allusions to her "escapade." Why had she spent even a second hoping Rosa would keep her mouth shut? Ginny's message was the most irritating. "Can't say I blame you. He really is a hunk. I only wish he'd turned his pretty blue eyes in my direction."

"Yeah, well that makes two of us," Lissa muttered, then listened to another message from her father.

"How come you told Steve there were no more spaces for booths? His idea is fantastic. Of course, I didn't tell him who the sandal belongs to, but I am helping him collect odd shoes from all over the island. The poetic justice of it tickles my fancy—Steve Jackson Jr. helping Madrona Cove earn the money that will keep Steve Jackson Sr. out of our hair! Talk to you later, honey. Give me a call the minute you get in, and I'll update you on everything Steve and I have planned. I like your guy, Liss. I like him a lot."

"He *is not* my guy!" she shouted, nearly loud enough for her father to have heard her in his trailer halfway up the hillside, almost a mile away. "I don't want a guy," she mumbled, unclenching her fists. "I don't need a guy. I need...sleep."

Quickly, she unplugged the phone, undressed, brushed her teeth and crawled into her berth. Maybe if she slept, she'd stop thinking about Steve, about what had happened, and about what *wasn't* going to happen in the future....

She had just dropped off, soothed by the gentle hiss of rain on the water, when something began bumping along the hull of the boat.

"Go away," she told it, but it continued to bump and pound. It would stop for a few minutes, then start up again. Each time, it seemed to be just a little farther away, but it wasn't going away fast enough to suit her. Obviously, a piece of driftwood caught by the tide had decided to snuggle up to her hull and it would stay there until she went out and got rid of it.

Grumbling with frustration and weariness, she pulled on her slicker over the T-shirt she slept in, stuck a rain hat on her messy hair and stomped on deck, grabbing a boat hook from its rack.

The wet deck felt cold under her bare feet as she made her way toward the bow, listening for the thump of the log. She only hoped she could reach it with the hook when she found it. Leaning over the rail, she checked for it, and drew in a sharp breath.

"Steve! What in the world are you *doing* down there?"

He lay over the bow of his boat, paddling with his hands. It was his boat that had been bumping into hers.

He looked up, his hair darkened with moisture, his mouth a grim, taut line and his eyes ablaze with temper. "F-freezing my ass off," he said, his teeth chattering so hard she could hardly make out his words. "T-trying to get this b-boat to the d-dinghy dock. Engine broke down." Obviously, the main boat dock was too high for even a tall man like him to climb out on, especially given his weakened condition.

Doggedly, he took two more strokes with his hands then grabbed one of her fenders, pulling himself along.

Trying to make sense of it all, Lissa asked, "Where are your oars?"

"One broke. Tried to paddle. Lost that one. F-fell overboard trying to g-g-grab it." His face was dead white, his eyes looked haunted, dark, as if he'd had about as much sleep as she had over the past couple of nights.

"Here," she said, finally showing a little sense. She thrust the boat hook at him. "Grab on. I'll tow you to the stern. You can get out there."

She could see how cold he was by the whiteness of his hands, the weakness of his grip and the way his

teeth continued to clack together. Even in July, thanks
to the constant churning of Seymour Rapids, it was too
cold to be in the ocean for more than a minute or two.
And with the rain and the fog, no wonder he was shivering so furiously. He had to be chilled to the bone.
She walked his boat to the low stern of hers, where she
stepped down and helped him scramble out.

As he got to his feet, he swayed, caught her shoulder,
and she stared at him in concern, steadying him with
her arms around him. "Go inside," she said, giving
him a gentle shove toward the door of the cabin. "I'll
take care of your boat."

Fear made her hands clumsy as she secured his runabout. The same fear sent her diving into the cabin,
down the companionway. Steve was still standing there
in jeans and a thin shirt so wet it clung to his body.
Great, wracking shivers shook him.

"Here," she said, "into the shower." She shucked
her slicker and dragged him through the door of the
head, closed it and swept the curtain around to keep
the cabinets dry. She turned on the hot water, uncaring
that she and Steve were both still clothed. He was completely soaked anyway, and she was only slightly less
wet from having manhandled him out of the boat.

Unhooking the handheld showerhead, she sprayed
warm water over his soaked hair, letting it splash down
over his shoulders and back. Moments later, she eased
him down to sit on the lid of the toilet. She hooked the
shower back up on its stand as hot water and steam
filled the small cubicle.

Crouching, she pulled off Steve's shoes, peeled off
his socks and rubbed his icy feet in her hands.

His teeth continued to chatter.

"How long were you out there?" she demanded,

shoving both his feet into the two inches of water in the bottom of the shower stall, and reapplying the hot water to his head, hoping he'd start warming up soon.

"S-s-since daybreak. Couldn't sleep. You weren't here. N-nothing else t-to do."

She didn't want to hear that. Didn't want to discuss it. "You went out without a jacket?"

"The weather was gr-great."

She unbuttoned his shirt and dragged it off him, rubbing his back and shoulders with a washcloth while directing the water with the other. "And you didn't head in the minute it started to deteriorate?"

"T-t-tried. Engine qu-quit."

"Stand up and take off your pants."

He tried to laugh though clattering teeth. "Y-you gonna spank me, Mom?"

"Oh, shut up," she snapped, unfastening his belt, then his zipper when his shaking hands were unable to cope. She skinned him out of his jeans and underwear, trying hard to pretend she was a nurse. As a pretense, it simply didn't work.

Nevertheless, she had to continue. She turned off the shower, slid the curtain back and grabbed one of her largest, thickest towels, wrapping it around his waist. Another, the same size, that nearly enveloped her, just managed to cover his back and shoulders.

Opening the door, she led him out and spun him around, rubbing his back briskly with the towel, reaching up to scrub at his hair just as vigorously. Still he shivered. Still his skin felt cold to the touch despite the hot water and friction. What should she do? What was the first-aid treatment for hypothermia?

Body warmth. Hot liquids, sugars.

She dragged him to her stateroom and flipped back

the sheet and thin blanket she used at this time of year. "Get in," she said, gesturing to her berth.

He turned and leered at her. "You're inviting me into your bed?" He actually managed a grin as he reached for her. "You really do something for a w-w-wet T-shirt, by the way."

"Into bed, Jackson. You're hypothermic. One of the symptoms is irrational behavior. You're in no shape for what you're thinking about. You need warmth." Oh, for Pete's sake! She shouldn't have to tell all this to a deep-sea diver with Antarctic experience! Maybe stupidity went along with irrational behavior. Yes. She was sure it did.

"B-bed with y-you would d-do it," he said.

She shoved him down, flipped the covers over him and reached under the sheet for the damp towel, which he relinquished by lifting his hips. She jerked the towel out quickly and rummaged in a locker for the down comforter she used in the winter.

With that over him, tucked in tightly, she rushed to the stove and put on the kettle to make hot chocolate.

While the kettle took its own sweet time boiling, she kept glancing over her shoulder through the doorway at Steve. He was still shivering. His teeth still clattered together. The water finally started bubbling, and she tossed an envelope of hot chocolate powder into a cup, stirred in the water and carried it to him.

"Sit up," she said. "Drink this."

His teeth jittered against the cup, but he downed most of it before thrusting it away. He lay back, vibrating her berth with the violence of his shivering. His eyes were closed, his lashes dark on his pale face. His lips looked bloodless.

"Oh, Lord!" Lissa whispered, setting the cup aside.

He was right. Her getting into bed with him would do it, would help warm him. She knew there simply was no choice. In one motion, she tore off her soggy T-shirt, slid under the covers with him and wrapped herself around him.

He shuddered, murmured something, and his arms came tightly around her.

She rubbed his back briskly until her arms ached and fell still from exhaustion.

"Tell me that story," he said, and she was glad to know his teeth had stopped chattering. "The one about the princess."

"She was in love with a handsome prince," Lissa said, desperately in need of something to keep her mind off the naked male flesh pressed against hers. "A dragon destroyed her castle and carried off her prince."

"Haven't you got that backwards?"

"Nope. The princess's belongings were all burned up except for a paper bag. She put that on and went out, intending to fight the dragon and rescue the prince."

"Hah! I knew you had it backwards."

"I did not. She set out to steal the prince back from the dragon, but it was a big, strong, dragon, too big and too strong for her."

"Ah, so the prince got to do the dragon slaying after all," he said, satisfaction clear in his tone.

Lissa laughed. "Don't bet on it. This is one tough princess we're talking about here. The prince was locked up in a cage in the dragon's lair. The princess knew she couldn't overcome the dragon physically, so she outsmarted him by sweet-talking him into doing just what she wanted. He was a terrible show-off, so he wore himself out trying to prove to her what a fierce dragon he was. When the dragon finally collapsed in a heap, she calmly walked into his cave and rescued the prince.''

"And they all lived happily ever after?" he said, and yawned prodigiously.

"Not exactly. The prince, who was a jerk, took one look at her and said he didn't want a princess whose hair was a mess and whose skin was all dirty, and who was wearing nothing but a paper bag. So she told him off and walked out. *She* lived happily ever after and I have no idea what happened to the prince.''

Lissa waited for Steve to make a comment. The only sound was a soft, gentle snore. With a smile, she continued to hold him, keeping him warm, glad she had rescued him, and equally glad he hadn't told her she was a mess and that he didn't want a sopping wet princess in a slicker and a rain hat and not much else.

He was a much nicer prince than the one Robert Munsch had written about. In a few moments, she felt sleep stealing over her, and thought she was dreaming a particularly graphic dream, until she realized something had wakened her, something undeniably hard and hot pressing against her thigh, and Steve's breath fanning her temple as he whispered her name.

"Lissa…"

"What…?" She tried to snuggle closer.

He tried to push her off. "God, Lissa, wake up. Listen to me. You'd better get out of this bed. Now.''

He held her in a half-sitting position, above him, his eyes glazed, his breath rapid. "Please, Lissa. Go. Now.''

She was silent, looking into his beseeching eyes. She tried to draw an even breath, but she couldn't, not with her body on fire. "I don't…know if I can," she whispered. Now she was the one who trembled. "I don't think I want to."

He groaned and slid his hands into her hair, his fingers tangling in her untidy curls, but she didn't care if he saw her looking a mess.

"Are you sure?"

"I'm sure," she said, leaning over him, kissing him, holding his face between her hands. "I want you, Steve."

"Lissa..." His voice shook, rumbling deep in his chest. His face took on a look almost of pain, but his gaze burned into hers as if seeking further reassurance.

"Kiss me," she said, and he did, then all she was aware of was the heat of his mouth on hers, the sexy, insistent thrust of his tongue, the seduction of it. She answered his demands, spreading herself atop him when he pulled her up over his chest. His hands cupped her buttocks, pressing her to him. Her blood pounded through her veins as need rose higher and higher.

"Lissa..." he groaned and she parted her legs, sliding them down the outsides of his thighs. His rigid erection pressed against her belly and she moved in a slow, steady rhythm that his hips repeated while his mouth continued to trace every inch of her face.

She strained to get closer, closer, no longer aware of anything but Steve, the scent of him, the feel of him, the taste of his skin and the rasping of his breath.

He slid her up his body until his mouth found her breasts, suckling while her back arched and her fingers raked his shoulders, caressed his cheeks, filtered through his hair. At last, at last, she brushed that tumbled lock off his forehead, tenderness and love pulsing through every inch of her.

He pushed the comforter back, gripping her body

with glorious, large warm hands. Holding her close, he rolled over so that he was atop her. He captured her legs with his, squeezing them together. She murmured a plea, aching to open to him, to accept him.

"Not yet," he whispered. "Don't rush this, sweetheart. It's too good to hurry."

As his touch stroked upwards, caressing the undersides of her breasts, her nipples hardened again, ached. His breath fanning over them did nothing to ease the sweet pain. Only his mouth could do that, but he denied her the relief she sought, finding other parts of her whose total sensitivity amazed her. Everywhere he touched her, kissed her, she burned and ached and throbbed until her whole body was one mass of need, need that swirled and built and finally focused low in her belly, where she felt empty, so empty, too empty.

She wanted... She needed... He must... Her soft moans became demands. Her body arched. She heard herself begging for his mouth, his lips, his tongue, for all the pleasures his touch promised.

And something deeper, some need, to be filled by him...

Heat scorched her body from within as the touch of his hands seared her skin. He slid off her, lying close by her side, his light stroking of her abdomen creating a fire that grew and grew until it threatened to incinerate her where she lay. He sat up and traced the shape of her body with his fingertips. His touch traveled down one leg to the tips of her toes.

"You're so beautiful," he murmured. "I've dreamed of doing this. Let me enjoy you. Let yourself enjoy me."

His sensual assault continued, as his fingertips walked lightly up between her breasts, over her throat, her ears, filtering through the thickness of her hair, massaging her scalp, then working their way down again. He spread his flat, hard palms over her, pressing her breasts together, his thumbs expertly massaging her nipples. His hands moved lower, spanning her waist, his fingers sliding under her hipbones, lifting her as his mouth traveled down her legs to her knees, parting them. Hot breath fanned up her thighs, then across the lower section of her belly as he knelt over her, surprising, teasing, tantalizing her with each kiss.

His ministrations sent wave after wave of incomparable sensation coursing through her, leaving her teetering on the verge of a shattering climax.

He touched her intimately with his fingers, parting her moist folds, and she arched into his caress. "Please, please," she said, determined to hold back, not to let this be like last time. "I need you. I—"

She broke off with a gasp as he bent and kissed her there, long and deep until she felt herself begin to shatter.

"I want…you…inside…me," she gasped, pulling his head up and away from her. She wrapped her hand around his hardness, feeling its heat, the pulsing of his need clearly matching her own.

"Me too." His voice came from far away. He looked at her, dazed, his face taut, a muscle bunching in his jaw. Then his eyes widened slightly, a blue glitter that held something approaching panic.

"Lissa… Oh, God…protection," he said, snatching her hand away from him and wrapping her in a tight embrace again, his big body trembling against hers, but not, this time, with cold. With heat, with desire, with restraint.

"Protection?" she echoed.

"Condoms, Lissa. Please, please don't tell me you don't have anything."

8

"I..." LISSA squeezed her eyes shut. "I...don't. I don't care that I don't. I...oh, yes! Yes I do! I mean, I have some."

She crawled off the bed, tottered naked on rubbery legs to the living quarters of the boat, reached up to a high locker and found the box Ginny had given her as a joke birthday gift.

Steve snatched it, fumbled it open, spilling a variety of brightly colored foil packets across the sheet.

He stared at her for a moment, then picked up two of the packets. "Lip-Lickin' Lemon?" he asked, "or Torrid Tomato?"

Lissa stared too. In addition to Lip-Lickin' Lemon and Torrid Tomato, there was Purple Passionfruit, Lime Lover and Golden Glow-Worm.

How many more there might have been in there, she couldn't count because suddenly she was gasping with laughter, smothering it in the hollow of Steve's shaking shoulders. "I'll kill her," she said. "I'll kill her for this!"

His arms wrapped tightly around her. "I won't," he said. "Whoever she is, she has my undying gratitude."

"For what? *Golden Glow-Worm?* Wouldn't any self-respecting man resent being likened to a worm?"

"Worms, I'll have you know, come in different shapes and sizes," he said, then stopped her laughter with his mouth. He rolled her over and kissed her deeply again and again, and passion once again flared up between them, returning in full force.

Lissa ached for him, wanting him totally. Her craving became an uncontrollable hunger.

"Please...please," she whispered again as she lifted her knees instinctively, let her legs fall apart in response to the knowing invasion of his fingers. "Now, Steve. Now!"

"Yes," he said, thrusting himself to his knees, rolling on the Torrid Tomato condom as she watched. "Yes," he said again as he pulled her up to him, thrusting his hips forward as their bodies finally, gratefully mated and became one.

Heaven, Steve thought. This was heaven. And not just because of a six-month dry spell during his Antarctic tour. This was heaven because it was Lissa moving under him, Lissa's scent surrounding him, Lissa's legs and arms wrapped tight around him. Lissa...

He'd never let her go. He held her tightly, trying to control the pounding need in his blood, wanting her satisfaction more than his own. Her hips made small, urgent circles, circles his hands could not contain however firmly he held her. He found her mouth, kissed her, heard the wonderful sound of her murmured pleasure, then felt her begin to come apart in his arms. Her head tossed back, rolling from side to side. Her hips lifted as her body became a stretched bow. He loved her that way, wanted the moment to go on forever, with her on the brink of climax, seeking a release only he could provide.

"Look at me," he said, and she opened her eyes, eyes filled with mystery, with the agony of almost achieving her goal, with the pleasure of waiting for it.

It was a pleasure he could deny neither of them any longer.

He lifted her hips again, plunged deeply, retreated, thrust again and again as Lissa cried out, her muscles rippling around him as she came. Her climax triggered his, drew everything from him, every sensation, every emotion, leaving him totally drained as he collapsed on her, and completely fulfilled as well.

With his last coherent thought, he took care to pull himself carefully from her, filled with a tender need to protect her to the end. Only vaguely was he aware of her drawing the warm down comforter over his back. Yet he was deeply, viscerally aware of the rightness of her snuggling closer into his arms as he slid down into sleep.

WHEN LISSA WOKE it was dusk. Steve leaned over her, teasing her nose with something that smelled vaguely like oranges. She nearly went cross-eyed trying to see what it was, but it was just a blur before her eyes.

"What's that?" she asked.

"Tangerine Tickler. Wanna try it?"

She pushed it away and sat up, blinking at the partially unrolled condom dangling from between his finger and thumb. Good grief! It had little...*feelers* on the end. And it really did smell like oranges. "They're scented as well as colored?"

His grin held pure mischief. "I think the word is *flavored,* sweetheart." He chuckled as Lissa felt her cheeks heat, and laid her back down, her head on his shoulder.

He ran the Tangerine Tickler over her face. "I love the way you blush."

"I don't."

"Don't blush, or don't love it?"

"Don't love it."

His expression softened from teasing laughter to tenderness that made her throat ache. "I love you, Lissa."

Her breath stopped. So did her heart. She managed to swallow. "Steve..." Her voice came out all tremulous and weak.

"It's okay." He kissed her softly. Then he kissed her not so softly as she responded. When he lifted his head, the Tangerine Tickler was nowhere to be seen. "I know you're not ready for that." he said. "You don't have to say it back. I just wanted you to know how I feel."

"But... It's too soon," she protested, on the verge of tears. "Falling in love this fast is insane."

He kissed her damp lashes. "Who gets to make up the falling-in-love schedule?"

"I don't know. I only know there's no such thing as fairy tales, and no such thing as happy endings."

"Just because you've never had one yet, doesn't mean they don't exist."

She knew her lips were trembling, and she tried to steady them. "I don't want to talk about it. I—" She broke off, burying her face against his shoulder again.

He combed his fingers through her hair. "What do you want, Lissa?"

"I don't know that, either."

"Then how about the Tangerine Tickler? Or maybe the Lip-Lickin' Lemon, or how about the Licorice Lollapalooza?"

Laughter she couldn't contain gurgled out. "There isn't one called that!"

"There is so. While you slept, I checked 'em all out, trying to decide which one we'd use next."

He picked it up from the locker beside her bed and showed her. "Who is the 'her' you're going to kill?"

"A friend." No way was she going to tell him which friend. He might decide he'd prefer a petite redhead with a wicked sense of humor. "She gave them to me for my birthday two years ago. She was trying to point out how mundane my life is."

"Was," he corrected.

Lissa knew she was blushing again. "I need a shower," she said. "I need something to eat."

He reached under the pillow and pulled out that damned Tangerine Tickler again, looking at her from under his thick lashes. "How about an orange?" he offered, then covered her mouth with his kiss.

LISSA WAS ONLY five minutes late getting to work. She'd left Steve sleeping in her bed and all she could think of was that eight hours from then, when she got off at 7:00, he might still be there.

She wanted him still to be there. She thought about him being there every morning when she arrived home from work, thought about sliding in with him, holding him, touching him, loving him.

In her imagination, he was there beside her on the sofa, yet instead of feeling joy, she felt sad and anxious as she sat watching an old movie on the television.

Only when the credits began to roll did she realize she had been so wrapped up in her thoughts about Steve, she hadn't even seen or heard a single thing in the movie.

One memory kept haunting her and filled her with pain. Steve was deep within her, moving powerfully, tirelessly, carrying her to greater and greater heights. And suddenly, there it was, a pure and simple truth she hadn't been able to escape then, and couldn't now: She wanted more from him, all of him, all he could give her. A baby to hold, a child to love. A home, a family.... Those things were the logical outcome of their physical and emotional union.

Yet the utter impossibility of fulfilling those needs and dreams brought tears to her eyes.

Suddenly, Steve was there, in body, not just in her imagination.

"Lissa? What's wrong?" He lifted her face and wiped her cheeks with the heels of his hands. His eyes radiated concern. When she buried her face against his chest, he tried to lift her chin.

"I don't want to look at you. I don't want you to look at me. I'm a mess."

"Well, at least you're not wearing a paper bag," he said, making her laugh despite her tears.

"That's better," he said. "Now tell me what's wrong."

"Nothing."

"*Tsk.* Just like a woman. Crying over nothing. Come on, I know better. If you're crying, you have a reason."

"I don't know who I am anymore."

"You're Lissa, the woman I love."

"Today," she said.

He tilted her face up and gave her a long, assessing look. "And tomorrow. For as many tomorrows as I can foresee."

"But that's the trouble. We can't, either of us, foresee the future."

He was silent for several moments. Then, "Ah, you're looking for guarantees."

She said nothing.

He locked his gaze with hers, as if he could see right into her soul. "I can't give you guarantees, Lissa."

"I know. So I'm not asking you to. And I can't give them, either."

"But you'd like me to. Is that the reason for your tears?"

She eased herself out of his arms. "Not really. I was just feeling weak and emotional for a minute. Wanting...something I'm better off not wanting."

"Such as?"

"Nothing I can put into words."

How could she explain the devastation she'd felt as a ten-year-old when her mother had dragged her away from her father, taken her out of the loving home she'd grown up in, taken her from all that was familiar? How could she tell him her mother had fallen for something as trite as a traveling salesman, one with great charm, good looks, and about as much staying power as a candle flame in a windstorm?

How could she make him see that she was like her mother, always attracted to the wrong kind of man? And she was like her in another way, too. It wasn't only that her mother had fallen out of love with Frank Wilkins—she'd fallen in and out of love with three more husbands since then. And Lissa's own unhappy romantic history mirrored her mother's. She'd had six intense relationships by the time she was thirty. Yet, as sure as she'd been that each one would last forever, she'd eventually gotten over her heartbreak and moved blithely on to the next one, having learned absolutely nothing, it seemed. Nothing except that she didn't want to bring children into the world so she could, by acting like her mother, tear apart the fabric of their lives.

Now, by falling for Steve, she was simply repeating a bad pattern.

"Try to put it into words," he urged.

She stood, moved restlessly away from him. "I don't want to talk about it, Steve."

He leaned back on the sofa, crossed one ankle over the opposite knee and eyed her. "Okay, then. Let's talk about something else."

Something in his expression sent a chill down her spine. "For instance?"

"For instance, exactly why you planted that ghost tape over my bed."

Lissa stood stock-still, groaned, and covered her eyes with one hand. "Oh, damn!"

"Yup," he said. "You've been busted." He didn't sound mad, only curious and amused.

Feeling sick, she wished she could feign ignorance, but she couldn't. She moved away, needing to put some space between them. He followed, giving her none.

All right. It was an issue between them and she knew it had to be addressed. So she tried, with a smile she knew could only be seen as phony.

"How did you know?"

His expression changed. "I didn't. I guessed. You had the opportunity. You have the legs—and the tattoo."

She backed away another step. "How did you know they were tapes?"

"I climbed into the attic through the hole you made and discovered them the first night you were away—which was, naturally, the first night I had an opportunity to hear them. You forgot to lock the bathroom door in my first room."

"Oh." Lissa's mouth went dry. "So why the Cinderella Search, if you know?"

His laughter was a short, unamused bark. "I was going to try to flush you out with that."

"It wouldn't have worked. I wouldn't have tried on the sandal."

"Exactly. And in refusing to play along, you'd have been admitting you didn't dare."

"Okay, now you know, so you don't have to do it."

"But I'm going to anyway."

"Why?"

"To earn cash for your fund."

Lissa closed her eyes for a second, then took three tottering steps before collapsing onto a chair. "Oh, God, Steve...I wish you'd forget the whole idea. Just leave."

He seemed unmoved by her distress. "No. I'm staying. I was set up and I want to know why. What did Rosa mean, when she said your dad had told you to 'make nice, not to make love'? What does that have to do with phony ghosts, with drawers opening and closing, hangers sliding from one end of the closet to the other?"

He crossed to her chair, leaned down, planting one hand on each arm of it, trapping her. "That's all I want from you now, Lissa. The reasons behind all this. I think you owe me that much."

"That's not all you wanted from me today in my bed," she snapped.

"No, it wasn't. And it won't be all I want from you in the future. But it is what I want now. Can't you trust me enough to tell me what's going on?"

She was torn with indecision. She loved him. What was love without trust? But her father, her friends, they were important, too, and they trusted her. For a long moment, she searched Steve's eyes, then drew in a deep breath and let it out slowly.

"I know why you're here, Steve," she said. "I—we've—known all along. John Drysdale, the real estate agent, told us someone was checking the place out this summer, with the intention of making a bid on it—Someone already in the resort management business. Why would you have come here, other than on your father's behalf?"

He frowned. "For a quiet vacation?"

"Please, don't try to deny it," she said. "You were the only stranger who booked this year. All the others are repeats from past years.

"When you made your booking, we realized you were the most likely potential buyer. Your father and his business aren't exactly low-profile. Neither are his methods. He sends in someone to look over a property he wants, discovers all its worst points, then makes his offer based on that knowledge. Okay, fair enough, I suppose that's a valid business practice. Nobody wants to buy a pig in a poke, and most vendors try to show a place in its best light. But we're not the vendors, and we don't want him to buy it at all."

"How would trying to scare me off with something as hokey as ghost stories prevent that?"

"It wasn't just ghost stories. There were the sounds, the drawers, the clothes. It would have scared *me!*"

"Didn't scare me, though. As soon as I found the tapes, I erased them so I could sleep without all that howling and moaning waking me up. The drawers I could live with." He grinned wolfishly. "I learned while living on shipboard that the best revenge for a practical joke is to pretend you don't notice it."

"It wasn't a practical joke." She explained about their wanting him to give his father a bad report. "We mean to buy this inn, Steve, but we won't be able to do it until after the festival."

Steve stood erect and backed up until he felt a chair against his knees and sank onto it as her words sank into him. "You've been toying with me, manipulating me, using me."

"No!" Her protest was vehement—and almost convincing. "Or, not through malice," she went on, actually admitting it. "Through desperation. But be honest, in coming here on an exploratory visit, pretending to be a legitimate guest, weren't you manipulating us? Even if we hadn't been on to you, you'd have found all sorts of faults and failures—things that are inevitable in an old building. What kind of report were you going to give him? One that would bring in a low bid, right?"

"Lissa—"

"So we gave you an excuse to make it a really low one. Or maybe none at all. Would your father want to buy a place full of ghosts and termites? Though the termites were just an inspiration on my part—I wasn't supposed to fall through the ceiling. But after I fell, I thought up the termites and figured you'd leave. But you didn't."

He looked at her steadily for a moment or two. He'd known she had secrets, known something was going on, but never in his wildest dreams would he have come up with a scenario like this. "I see. That must have been disappointing for you."

"Steve…" Lissa hated to beg, but for this, she'd do it. "We don't want your father or anyone else to buy the inn because we're almost in a position to do it ourselves. This year, with what we make from the festival, we should have just enough, but only if you don't come in with a bid before our option runs out.''

"So, in order to regain the inn, your father asked you to make nice with me? Keep me happy, maybe? What was that supposed to accomplish?''

"If...if we don't make enough to cover our bid, and your family takes over, Dad—we all thought—it would be to our advantage to have you in our corner.''

"We, we, *we*,'' he said, leaping up and pacing away from her. "You're the one who seduced the hell out of me when you saw I wasn't about to leave. You're—''

"No!'' she cried, rising just as swiftly. "I didn't seduce you! I tried to resist you, but—''

"Garbage,'' he snapped, crowding in on her so close she felt the heat of his body. It would have melted her, but for the anger she saw simmering through him. "You learned a lot from that little story of yours, didn't you? Made it a pattern for your life, maybe? You couldn't slay the dragon by fair means, so you used foul. You outsmarted me, played me for a fool, made me show off and exhaust myself trying to prove to you what a wonderful dragon I was until I was too weak to resist you.''

"You're crazy! It wasn't like that at all. It—''

"Maybe I *was* crazy, but I'm not anymore. I'm beginning to see straight. *You're* the one who's trying to keep anyone else from buying the inn.''

"Not just me,'' she protested. "Us. We, the committee in charge of fund-raising. The whole town.''

"It wasn't the whole town that got into my blood, who kissed me till my eyes crossed, who made love to me like a sorceress. God!'' Steve exploded, clamping his hands over her shoulders, unable to hide his roiling emotions from her.

She winced and he let her go, turned and strode away from her, coming to a halt near the fireplace. There, he spun and faced her again from a safer distance. "And you called *me* an opportunist!"

"I didn't know you then, Steve. Didn't care about—"

"Don't bother, Lissa." He cut off her words with a chopping motion of his hand. "Your explanations are specious just because they come from you. I don't like being manipulated. I don't like being used, and that's exactly what you've done to me from the very beginning, you and those big brown eyes of yours, that sexy body. How do I know you didn't crash through the ceiling on purpose, just to intrigue me?"

"I didn't!" she shouted. Then, as if remembering where she was, and that it was the middle of the night, she modulated her tone. "You've got it all wrong!" she went on, pleading now. "Remember, when this all started, I hadn't even met you, hadn't come to know you. I hadn't learned to...care about you."

"And you want me to believe that you do now?"

"Yes." Her voice was little more than a whisper. Those damned brown eyes brimmed with unshed tears. They were nearly his undoing, but he steeled himself, let his anger feed on itself, feeling it swell in his chest.

"You don't care about me now," he accused, "and you didn't care about me then."

"Not then, no. I admit that. All I cared about was the inn and my dad. He desperately wants it back. Steve, please understand. It was in his family for years. His father lost it in...in a pinochle game of all things, to one of his rich guests who then made him manager.

The inn was my dad's home from the time he was born. He thought of it as his baby from the age of twenty when his father was killed in a plane crash and he took over managing it. He made it what it is now. Or, what it used to be, what the entire town knows he can make it again, once he's in a position to take charge. I'll do anything to help him achieve that goal.''

Steve stood silent, digesting what she'd said. "Obviously, then, you should be able to understand my doing what my father wants me to do, right?''

Miserably, she nodded, so miserably, he almost forgave her, almost told her the truth, that he wasn't there on his father's behalf. "Yes. I suppose so," she said. "Your father runs a successful business. I know he needs to find opportunities to expand his area of operations. But not here, Steve. Please, that's all I'm asking of you, not here!''

"Why not here? Because you don't want him to? Aren't you the one who told me no one can have everything they want?''

"This isn't just for me. It's for my dad. It's important to him in a way that it can't possibly be important to yours. The inn is all he knows, Steve, all he wants.''

"And you're such a dutiful daughter, you'd even sleep with the enemy to get him what he wants. How altruistic of you, Lissa.''

He watched anger replace sorrow in her eyes, watched her chin come up and color flare in her cheeks. He'd never wanted her more than at that moment. But to take her now, to make love to her before he sorted through what he really felt for her after these revelations would have been wrong. For both of them.

Her anger was short-lived. "No. Not altruistic in the least," she said, dropping down onto a chair, defeat in the droop of her shoulders. "If your father's company gets the inn, there's no guarantee they'll do as the last two owners have done and let my dad store his old junk in the attic. If it has to be moved out, he'll expect me to move off my boat and into a house where there's room for it—and him. That's what he wanted when I first came back. It would take two of us to pay the rent, but I don't want to have to live with him, or his moldy old furniture that he keeps telling me is my 'heritage.' It's a heritage I have no use for. Nor do I want to live in a house. I have my boat. It's my freedom. I love it. I can't give it up."

"Even if your moving into a house with him would make your father happy?"

"That's unfair," she said. "Yes, I want Dad to be happy, but not at the expense of my own happiness. And unless he gets his job and his life back, I can't have mine back."

"So when he's happily managing this place again, you're free to go. Go where, Lissa?"

"I told you. I want to put my boat to work. I want to run tours. Oh, God, is it so hard to understand that I just want my dad to have what he wants, so I can live my own life again?"

Right. A life in which she'd have no use for furniture, no use for a house—a home.

Those two statements answered a lot of questions for him. Lissa Wilkins had no use for permanency. It wasn't just the fear that she'd be left high and dry and hurting she'd been crying over. It was the fear of losing her freedom. If her dad got the inn back, then she'd be gone on the morning tide.

Why it surprised him, he didn't know. Why it hurt him so, he didn't want to think about. And he'd thought she was crying because he couldn't offer her any iron-clad guarantees. Bull. She was the one who couldn't do that.

It struck him then that she hadn't said she'd been crying because of *his* inability to provide guarantees, but because of *their* inability. She didn't believe that his love, or her own for him, could create the kind of guarantees something in her yearned for—something she worked so hard at squelching. After all, she didn't believe in happy endings.

WEDNESDAY, THURSDAY, Friday... Where was Steve? She looked at the register each night she came on duty, but he hadn't checked out. She'd had dinner with her dad and Rosa at Chuckles on Thursday. He hadn't been there. She'd sat in the lounge for more than three hours after arriving at work, and he didn't come downstairs. On Friday, someone mentioned he'd been fishing and had donated three salmon for the community barbecue during festival weekend.

Okay, he was avoiding her. That should have suited her just fine. It didn't. She ached to see him, yearned for just one more chance to make him understand. But he gave her no opportunity. On Friday night, she even considered slipping upstairs and knocking on his door, but pride held her back. Pride, mixed with a hefty dose of fear. As long as she hadn't heard him say it was over, a small, secret part of her could pretend. Pretending was all right, wasn't it? Just sometimes? After all, a little fantasy went a long way toward soothing an unsoothable pain.

Saturday morning, after an exhausting night trying to sleep, she gratefully turned the desk over to a sour-faced Pete. He had still not forgiven her for calling him in early when she'd needed to escape. He'd made her week even more miserable than it had to be. Hell, he'd made much of the past two years miserable for her. This morning though, he was in an even fouler mood than normal because when she left, she wouldn't be back for two full weeks and he'd have to find a different whipping girl on whom to vent his spleen. Gertie, the relief desk clerk would be taking her place. Lissa could almost laugh, since nobody, but nobody, intimidated Gertie. Especially not Pete.

Thank goodness the festival was the following weekend. The take would be tallied up, and maybe, just maybe, Pete would be out of a job. As, of course, would she. She couldn't wait.

No sooner had Lissa returned to the boat than the phone started ringing. The exhibitor on the other end was demanding running water in his booth. By the time he hung up, she was envisioning fifty garden hoses strung together, snaking across the park. Hoo-boy!

The phone rang again immediately, and Lissa soothed another worried exhibitor. The minute that caller hung up, there was hammering on the door. In quick succession she dealt with the problems of six people, most of whom wanted to change the location of their particular booths.

"Traffic flow," said Hank Marsden, a regular exhibitor who created wrought-iron sculptures. "You have to think of traffic flow, Lissa. If people enter the park here—" with a grimy fingernail he jabbed at the plan spread out on the coffee table "—they'll have spent all their money in these eighteen other booths before they ever get to mine." She'd had this argument with him twice before, and moved his booth both times. This year she meant to stand firm.

Someone else knocked on the door. "Come in!" she called, hoping it was another participant who also hated his or her location and would be willing to trade with Hank.

She had no idea if the man who trotted down the companionway still intended to be have a booth. There was nothing on her master plan that said he did. But suddenly her mouth went dry.

Steve's question echoed in her mind. *Who gets to write the falling-in-love schedule?*

She'd like to ask him who got to write the falling-*out*-of love schedule. Obviously, *he* did. He looked bright-eyed, well rested, and not in the least disturbed. She just wished he'd tell her his secret. Then, on the other hand, maybe she didn't want to know it. Maybe it was simply the fact that he had never been in love with her, had merely tossed the word around as casually as most men did in order to get what they wanted. It took her a moment to remember he hadn't said that word until after he'd gotten what he wanted.

She would dearly have liked to ask him what he wanted now, but couldn't speak. She managed a courteous nod and waved him to the settee. He listened as she and Hank continued to wrangle over booth locations.

"May I make a suggestion?"

"Please do." She kept her tone cool.

"If Hank's booth were here," he said, tapping the paper with the tip of a pencil, "his customers could back right in here." He indicated a position at the rear of the parking area. "We could tape it off and mark it as a loading zone."

Hank leaned over the paper, brightening. "Right.

There'd only be about ten feet to carry things. But is there a path through the underbrush there?''

Lissa shrugged. "If there isn't one now, there's sure to be by the end of the festival. If," she added, "*if* I can persuade the renter of booth twenty-three to trade with you." She shuffled through the sheaf of papers that should have been in order, but no longer were.

"No problem," Steve said. "That's my booth, and I'm more than happy to trade if it makes things work out for you."

She stared at him, trying to read his expression, but somehow he'd managed to hide his thoughts and feelings, as if he'd pulled the shades down over them.

"Great!" Hank said, pumping Steve's hand. "You've got yourself a deal, buddy. What are you selling, anyway?"

"Chances," Steve said. "The same thing as I'm taking," he added in a lower voice.

"And now, gentlemen," Lissa said quickly, "if you'll forgive me, I worked on this stuff all night and haven't had any sleep yet." Not for the world would she admit she hadn't slept because thoughts of Steve had kept her awake. "I'm going to unplug my phone, put a Do Not Disturb sign on my door, and go to bed."

Hank, now that he was satisfied, became contrite and apologized profusely for the intrusion as he wrote out his check for the balance of his booth rental.

Steve said nothing, only opened the door for Hank and let him out. Then he closed it after him and stood looking at Lissa.

Lissa stared fixedly at the blank sheet of paper she'd torn off a writing tablet, then at the black felt marker in her hand, watching it shake.

"Lissa, look at me." Steve's voice poured over her like warm honey.

She didn't look at him, but finished printing DO NOT DISTURB, then carefully set the pen down. Steve took the sign and fixed it to the outside of the door, which he closed firmly and locked from the inside. Lissa hovered halfway between the saloon and the galley, halfway between telling him to go and begging him to stay.

He approached her slowly. When his fingers touched her cheek, she flinched, but didn't back away. "What do you want here?" she asked. "You sure as hell don't need a booth. You already know whose tattoo you saw, who fell through your ceiling. You don't have to try that sandal on 'every girl in the kingdom' as your signs say, to find your princess. Haven't you figured it out yet, Steve? There *are* no more princesses in this world. And no princes."

"How about dragons?"

"Lots of those."

"And you want to slay them all. All by yourself."

"And you think, in running this booth, in helping us make money, you're going to prove to me you can slay a few for me?"

"I don't want to have to prove anything to you, Lissa, but I've advertised it," he said. "Promised prizes. So I plan to go through with it."

She clenched her fists. "All right. Go through with it. Since you've also advertised that all proceeds will go to the community fund, you have no need to be here. You don't have to pay me rent."

"I have a need to be here," he said levelly. "A need to talk to you."

"What about? Didn't you say all you had to Tuesday night?"

"I wasn't being fair to you Tuesday night. You've been fighting for the inn a long time. I know that. I also know you weren't using me or trying to distract me with sex. Okay, maybe it took me awhile to realize it and decide what to do. I never said I was a quick study."

"You said you loved me, Steve, yet you were willing to jump to conclusions about my motives the minute you found out I'm against your father's buying the inn."

"I do love you, and I was wrong to jump to those conclusions. I also have to tell you that as far as I'm aware, my father has never heard of Madrona Cove, the Madrona Inn, or even Quadra Island. He didn't send me here to check things out preparatory to his making a bid. If there's another buyer in the picture, I don't know who it is. The only reason I came here is because a friend recommended it. He used to come here with his family when he was a kid. You might even remember him. Jake Wallace?"

"I remember Jake."

"We were on shipboard together this past winter."

Lissa backed away, searching his eyes, looking for truth. About Jake, she believed him, but about the rest of it, she was still unsure. It was hard to give up a preconceived notion. And if it wasn't Jackson Resorts who was interested, then who could it be?

As if he sensed her confusion, Steve said quietly, "You can either believe me or not. The choice is yours. That's what I meant when I said I was taking chances.

I'm taking a chance on something I think will be good for both of us.''

In other words, the ball was in her court.

9

LISSA MET his steady gaze, struggling to speak past the tension in her throat. Finally, she was able to whisper, "I...believe you."

He took a step closer to her.

"I wasn't lying, Steve."

"When you said you cared about me?"

She nodded. He took another step toward her. "I want more than that," he said.

She couldn't answer him. Not in words. She took a step toward him, and then, suddenly, the world was right-side-up again as they tightly embraced.

His kiss was deep and dark and full of promise. His eyes, when he lifted his head, were filled with love and compassion. "You need sleep," he said, lifting her off her feet and carrying her through the galley, then into her room. "And I mean to stand guard and make sure you get it."

He laid her down on her berth. She kept her arms around his neck. "Uh, do you think you could stand guard from a prone position?"

He laughed and slid his length against hers. "I thought you'd never ask."

"Maybe," she said, a few moments later, "I'm not as tired as I thought I was."

"Well, in that case," he said, rolling to one side and scooping up a few of the packets still strewn across her bedside table. "What will it be, Pink Peppermint-Stick, Cinnamon Sizzler, or Chocko-Cocko?"

"What? You made that up!"

"Did not."

She read the label on the brown foil. He hadn't made it up. They collapsed together, giggling, then kissing, and Lissa found herself wondering exactly how many different descriptions the manufacturers of those condoms had come up with. And how many they'd go through while Steve's vacation lasted.

She didn't dare think of the time to follow.

HE LOOKED GOOD with a hammer in his hand, Lissa decided Monday morning. Wielding it, he looked even better. The muscles in his back rippled in the sunlight as he nailed the roof of his booth in place, using boards painted to look like the stone blocks of a castle—the one Cinderella lived in. As she watched him, Lissa paused in her work of helping Caroline set up her booth nearby.

"Hey, you're supposed to be helping me, not gobbling up the competition with your eyeballs."

Lissa swung around and grinned sheepishly at Caroline, who grinned back. "Though I have to admit," Caroline continued, "he is good to look at. Are you bringing him to the committee lunch today? He deserves it. He's worked as hard as any of the rest of us."

Lissa nodded. "He's coming." If he hadn't been, she wouldn't have attended. It scared her, how much she needed to be near Steve. She hated to be out of range of his voice, not to be able to reach out and know he'd be there to touch. It even scared her that she sensed he felt exactly the same about her, that his feelings were genuine, deep, and for the long haul. They hadn't discussed the future, not really, but it was there between then, unspoken, yet almost tangible. One way or another, they would be together.

AN HOUR LATER, they returned to her boat to shower away the sweat and grime of their morning's labor. "I suppose," he said, sliding his wet body against hers in the small cubicle, "we could have gone to my room to shower."

She pushed herself up against him. "Isn't this more fun?"

He sat on the lid of the commode and pulled her astride him. "Do you want to be late for lunch?" she asked.

"Hell, yes!"

She gasped as he slipped inside her, and rocked against him as powerful tremors of pleasure shuddered through them. They both climaxed fast and hard, and when it was over, Lissa couldn't move. She could only nestle close to her lover, her head on his shoulder, her arms around his back.

They missed lunch altogether, but made it to the inn in time to walk in on an altercation between Pete and a well-dressed woman in her mid-fifties, who appeared to be unwilling to take no for an answer.

Pete planted his pudgy hands on the desk. "I'm telling you, lady, if someone was supposed to have made reservations for you within the last two days, there's no record of it here and—" He broke off, spotting Lissa. "You!" he said. "I bet it was you. Did you promise this lady a room and forget to make a note of it?"

Lissa took a step back and bumped into Steve, whose

arms came around her from behind. "No," she said. "If you recall, Pete, I haven't been on duty for the past two days."

"Then it was probably on your last night. You screwed up, Lissa. Admit it."

"I did no such thing!"

"You think you can get away with anything, don't you, just because your family once owned this dump? Well, let me tell you, miss, your days here are numbered and—"

Frank and Rosa came out of the dining room just then. "What's all this bellowing?" Frank asked. "We have guests in the inn, I might remind you." His gaze lit on the woman. His shoulders went back. His chest went out. He sucked his belly in. Lissa stared at him.

"This is none of your business, Frank Wilkins. You're not in charge here anymore, remember?" Pete's contempt for Frank was obvious.

"Please, it was clearly a mistake," the lady said. "I'm sure I can find a bed-and-breakfast somewhere nearby. Can anyone suggest one?"

Pete snorted. Frank rubbed his chin and continued to gaze at the woman as if he'd never seen one before.

Silence hung loud in the lobby for a moment until Lissa spoke, "I'm sorry, Mrs...?"

"Forsythe. Loretta Forsythe." She smiled at the group and Lissa noted that her gaze lingered on Steve. But then it focused intently on Lissa's father, and she seemed just as taken with him as he was with her. She actually patted her perfectly coiffed dark gold hair and lowered her lashes as she looked at Frank from under them and smiled coquettishly.

Rosa, Lissa could see by her bristling, noticed that little detail, too.

"I'm sorry, Mrs. Forsythe," Lissa repeated, "but we're preparing for our town's birthday bash next weekend, and there's absolutely no accommodation to be had on the island. I wish we could help you, but..." She shrugged. Her apology was false. She didn't like the way her father was acting. How could he be such a dork, ogling the stranger, hurting Rosa this way?

"She can have my room," Steve said, right out of the blue.

Lissa gaped at him. "But—" He squeezed her shoulder as he stepped around her. "I've been invited to spend the rest of my vacation aboard a boat in the marina, so I was planning on checking out today, anyway. That is, Mrs. Forsythe, if you don't mind three flights of stairs and antique furnishings. You'll be sleeping in a genuine sleigh bed."

She beamed. "Why, thank you, Mr...?"

"Jackson." He grinned. "Steve Jackson. And this is Frank Wilkins."

"Mr. Wilkins," she cooed. "I'm *so* pleased to meet you." She smiled, blue eyes blazing with what appeared to be genuine delight. "I understand your family built this inn. I bought a fascinating book about Madrona Cove on the ferry and read it all the way from Horseshoe Bay to Vancouver Island."

"I'm delighted to meet you, too," Frank said, taking both her hands in his. "My mother wrote the original history of the inn, then I added a few chapters later. This is my daughter, Lissa, who I hope will bring the book up to date for its next printing."

Not wanting to comment on that, and wanting to drag her father back to reality, Lissa said, "And this is Rosa—" She broke off. Rosa was gone.

"I'll go and pack," Steve said. "It won't take me

long, Mrs. Forsythe. I'm sure you'll want to get settled.'' He grinned. "I bet Frank could find you a comfortable chair in the lounge, and possibly a drink.
Right, Frank?'' Without waiting for a reply, he took
the stairs two at a time.

"I don't have any chambermaids on at this time of
day,'' Pete said, sullen and uncooperative. "What do
you expect me to do, climb those stairs myself and fix
up the room?''

Lissa slid a glance over his bulk. Pete had never
climbed a stair that she'd ever heard of. She wasn't
sure he was able, which was why he'd never taken the
option of occupying the top floor, as was the manager's
right. Instead, he'd taken the best cabin and ate in the
dining room. And ate and ate and ate...

"Liss'll take care of it, won't you, honey?'' her father said. "She spent most of her high-school vacations
chambermaiding for me when I managed the place, and
I'm sure she hasn't forgotten how. Now, let's see about
that drink, Mrs. Forsythe.''

"Call me Loretta,'' she said. "And I'll call you
Frank. I have a feeling we're about to become very
good friends.''

As Lissa headed by on the way to the stairs, the
dining room doors squeaked and she saw Rosa's
stricken face peering out through the crack.

Damn her father! She couldn't believe the way he
was acting.

"Thanks a lot,'' she said to Steve, slamming a stack
of bedding down on the dresser.

He stared at her. "What's eating you?''

"You. Giving your room up to that...that middle-
aged femme fatale! My father's gone into orbit over
her, and poor Rosa's heartbroken. Couldn't you see

he'd gone gaga over her the minute he laid eyes on her?''

"Rosa? Your dad and Rosa are an item?"

"They were. Till you interfered. If that woman had been forced to go elsewhere for a room, Dad wouldn't have become instantly infatuated and—"

He caught her in a bear hug, winked, then dropped his lashes to half-mast. "And you wouldn't have the sexiest roommate in town. I saw this as a serendipitous opportunity. I give up my room for a lady in distress, and get to legitimately spend my nights aboard your boat. Of course," he added with another wink, "I'll put my gear in one of the aft cabins just in case you want your reputation protected."

Lissa sighed and snuggled against him, unable to resist. And of course he hadn't known about her dad and Rosa. He hadn't been here long enough to have noticed all the little nuances everyone else could see.

"I don't think I have a bit of reputation left. There probably isn't a soul in Madrona Cove who'll believe you're sleeping in an aft cabin."

He kissed her. "Do you mind?"

She laughed. "The only thing I'd mind was if you really did want to sleep back there."

"ROSA!" Lissa exclaimed as she opened the door of her boat two days later. Tears streaked down Rosa's face. "What's wrong?" As if she didn't know. "Come sit down. I'll make some tea."

Rosa had herself under better control by the time Lissa returned with the tea. She sniffed and sat up straight in her chair. "Your father's fallen in love with that woman."

"Oh, Rosa, maybe he's just going through a midlife crisis."

"Hah! He left mid-life behind fifteen years ago. Trouble is, I'm older than he is and now he's set his sights on someone younger. He's been with her almost constantly for the last two days. They've had every meal together, he's spent hours up in her room—talking, supposedly, but I know better. Frank Wilkins isn't that much of a talker. He's more of a—" She broke off, turning her face away.

Lissa poured two cups of herbal tea and put one in Rosa's trembling hands.

"I never asked, because I didn't think it was my business, but well, you and Dad...for years I've wondered why you didn't marry."

"I couldn't." Rosa lifted a tragic face to Lissa. "I was married till just a couple of years ago. My husband was in a home. He died the month before your dad had his stroke. I was free then, but Frank wouldn't marry me 'cause he was sick and didn't think he had anything to offer me."

"He's not sick now, Rosa."

"But he still doesn't think he has anything to offer me." She sipped her tea, then set it down. "I wonder what he thinks he's got to offer that woman? Or maybe he doesn't have to offer her anything. She looks rich, doesn't she? Maybe she's offering him something he can't refuse. Maybe she's going to buy the inn for him or something. How can I compete with that? I'm sixty-four. I'll have my old-age pension in a couple of months. But it sure won't make me rich. It won't help me buy the inn for him."

"*We're* going to buy the inn, Rosa. This festival is going to be the best one ever. Just you wait. And when

Dad's reinstated as manager, you and he will move into those upstairs rooms—together.''

"Nice try, Lissa, but don't hold your breath."

IT WAS THURSDAY at ten in the morning when John Drysdale, the Realtor, sauntered up to Lissa and dropped his bombshell. Wearing brightly polished shoes, a blue suit and a red tie, with his professionally styled hair perfect as always, he looked completely out of place amid the bustle of jeans-clad townsfolk rushing around getting ready for the festival.

"Well," he said. "You got till five-thirty Saturday to make good on your offer."

She dropped the archery target she was nailing to a post. She also dropped the hammer. It landed on her toe. She scarcely felt the pain. "What are you talking about?" she demanded, knowing perfectly well what he meant.

"The seventy-two-hour clause. It's been invoked. Someone made an offer as of 5:30, yesterday afternoon. I got over here to tell you as soon as I could."

"It can't be true! You're kidding, aren't you?"

He shook his head. Lissa closed her eyes tight. She didn't know why her brain kept insisting on denying the truth. Her stomach already knew it. It lay so heavily within her she was one big ache. Her head spun. How could this be happening? Steve had said... *No!* Her every instinct told her he hadn't lied. He loved her. She had to trust him. It was not his father who'd put in the offer. Someone had. *But who?*

She didn't realize she'd said it aloud until Drysdale spoke cheerfully, cutting into her chaotic thoughts, "You know I can't tell you that, Lissa. But if you and your committee can come up with the money before 5:30 Saturday, you're in. If not, you're out.''

How could he sound so uncaring, so unfeeling? Didn't he know what this meant to the community, to her father? "But John! You know we won't have the tally from the festival until Sunday at the earliest! You can't do this to us!"

"It's not personal, Lissa. It's business. I represent the vendor. I have to accept the offer of anyone who comes to me with the cash."

"But we'll have it!" she protested. "We will!"

He shrugged. "Maybe so, but if you don't have it by 5:30 Saturday, it'll be too late. Sorry, Lissa. See you."

"Wait!" she said, taking two running steps after him. "John, don't...don't tell anyone else about this. Not yet. Please. Not with the festival so close." Was there a chance, some small, remote chance, they could pull it off?

He shrugged. "No skin off my nose. I don't want to rain on your parade. Just so long as you realize I'll need a check by 5:30 Saturday." He paused. "Certified."

She closed her eyes again. When she opened them, John Drysdale was gone.

Twenty minutes later, she sat staring in dismay at the figures Debra Hix, treasurer of the committee, showed her. Debra, a canny businesswoman, owner of the hardware store, and successful accountant in her spare time, knew what she was talking about. Her gray eyes gazed compassionately into Lissa's as she ran a hand through her short, crisp hair. "I don't see any way, honey."

"Not even if we collect the cash from all the community-sponsored booths just before five on Saturday?''

Sadly, Debbie shook her head. ''It won't be enough. We'll still need the percentage we get from all the other booths, and even then, it'll be a squeaker. And we won't see any of that for at least three days. Most of it will take a couple of weeks to get to us.''

''Then it's game over.''

Debbie studied the figures, tapped the paper with her pencil, and said, ''Maybe we could try for a loan again. Damn! If the hardware store wasn't so heavily mortgaged, I'd offer to put it up as collateral, but...''

Lissa hugged her. She knew how hopeless it was to try to get a loan. They'd tried. But as a group, they had no assets. The bank wouldn't talk to them.

''Thanks, Deb. I'd do the same with *Lady,* only she's got a mortgage as big as some small countries' national debt. I just don't know how I'm going to tell my dad.''

Debbie nodded with understanding. ''Then don't. Not yet. Let him enjoy as much of the festival as he can. Deals have fallen through before, you know, and until the last minute of those seventy-two hours has run out, we really haven't lost.''

Unconvinced, Lissa left the hardware store.

All she wanted now was to crawl into Steve's arms, have him hold her, comfort her, tell her it would be all right. The depth of her need for him scared her.

SHE WENT to him anyway.

She found him exactly where she'd expected to. ''I'll have a kid down here,'' he was saying as she approached his booth. She couldn't see him, so he must be crouched behind the counter. ''He'll hook a shoe on each time someone puts a line down, but every third shoe will be that Birkenstock sandal I told you about, since every ticket buys three chances."

The woman he addressed laughed. "Since you know who was in the attic, darling, why does it matter who owns the sandal?"

Lissa stopped in her tracks. *Darling?*

"It doesn't," he said. "but someone has to win the grand prize, Mom, since I've already offered it."

Lissa stared at Loretta Forsythe's elegant, silk-bloused back. *Mom?*

Her ears hummed so loud she almost missed Steve's next words. "It may as well be the woman who fits the sandal, in true Cinderella fashion. Dad's offered a two week, all-expenses vacation. Someone might as well enjoy it."

"Too bad it's *not* your Lissa's sandal, Stevie. The hot-springs resort would make a good place for a honeymoon. Almost as good as the Madrona Inn."

Steve thumped something under the counter, then stood, his normal grin on his face. "You let me worry about that, Mom. The last thing I want is— *Lissa!*"

She stared at him, reading the guilt on his face, the shock, the truth.

Still, she had to say it. "*Mom?* This woman is your mother?"

"Yes." He scrambled out from behind the counter. "Lissa, God, don't look at me like that! Please, listen to me. I can explain. I—"

"Go to hell, Steve Jackson," she said, and her words seemed to stop him in midstride. "Just go to hell. I was a total idiot to believe you, to trust you. Well, never again." She laughed, her voice cracking. "And to think I came to you for comfort when I heard someone had invoked the seventy-two hour clause! Okay, fine. You've won. We won't have enough money to make good our bid for several days after that. I hope you and your family enjoy your new acquisition."

She spun on her heel and marched across the park, seeing no one, hearing no one. It took her all of five minutes to unplug everything, cast off and head *Boss Lady* out of Madrona Cove. Okay, so she was running away. She knew it, and she didn't care.

How many dragons was one woman supposed to try to slay in a lifetime? She'd taken on her last one and she'd lost. Funny how she'd never before noticed how much a dragon could resemble a snake.

If only she didn't have to go back to the Cove for the festival, Lissa thought. She'd just keep right on traveling. Desolation Sound would make an appropriate destination, wouldn't it, given the state of her emotions?

But her father would be devastated enough to learn of the loss of his last shot at regaining the inn. She couldn't desert him when he needed her the most. Still, she needed some time to herself before the festival began. She'd anchor out until Saturday morning. She was entitled to time and space to lick her wounds.

HE MADE A BEAUTIFUL Prince Charming. Steve looked better in purple tights and puffy pantaloons than Lissa could possibly have imagined. The knee-length pants, gold with royal-purple insets, matched his ermine-trimmed gold crown, and his gold tunic molded to his chest like paint.

A parade of hopeful Cinderellas flocked to his royal booth. He ushered each one to a gilt throne, seated her as if she were a real princess, and handed her a fishing pole. Then he knelt before her and tried to fit each shoe she caught to her foot. Most didn't fit, but each visitor left happily, dizzily overwhelmed by the consolation prize—one of his exquisite kisses.

She shouldn't have come back. She'd realized that the minute she finished tying up the boat and heard the festivities carrying on as if no one had missed her. Conscience, loyalty, duty and concern about her father had forced her to haul up anchor and chug back to the Cove.

Well, she was here now. And she was damned if she'd let Steve, or anyone else, see how shattered she was inside. Strolling around the park, she checked on most of the booths, acting like the coordinator she was supposed to be. She dealt with minor problems, laughed and joked and hid her pain deep inside. When she came to Steve's booth, though, she sailed right on past. No one there even seemed to notice her presence.

"Hey, Caroline, could you use a break?" she asked, approaching the kissing booth.

"Wow, could I ever!" Caroline patted her lips with her fingertips. "They're beginning to wear out. Take over—it's all yours."

Lissa put her heart and soul into every kiss she sold, breaking Caroline's rule of no touching except for lips. Soon a line as long as Steve's had formed in front of the kissing booth. Money piled up in the cash drawer. Lissa's head spun with weariness and her lips ached from overuse. Hey, she thought groggily, maybe they'd take in enough from this booth alone to meet the deadline.

Caroline came back after her lunch break, took one look at the overflowing cash box and stepped in to help take up some of the slack.

"Holy cow!" she muttered to Lissa between patrons. "I wish I'd agreed to full-body contact years ago. We'd have had that inn long ago! I hope you can stick around for the rest of the afternoon. Then, if Jase comes over, I can tell him the lineup's for you."

Caroline flung herself wholeheartedly into a kiss that left her client staggering, as Lissa finished with her own. Then she looked up at the next man in line, and saw a tilted golden crown and a pair of blue eyes glaring into hers.

"Where the hell have you been?" he said in a low voice, but obviously furious. "You took off with everything I own, you know. I didn't have so much as a razor! And your dad's been going nuts, worrying about you."

She couldn't have cared less about his razor. He

174 The Cinderella Search

looked perfectly shaved. "Well, he'll have something a whole lot worse to worry about soon, won't he?" she said, looking pointedly at her watch, which read 1:35.

"Lissa, if you hadn't—"

"Hey, you gonna pay your money and get your kiss, or you gonna stand there yacking?" asked the guy behind him.

Steve glanced over his satin shoulder and said, "There's another kisser."

"Yeah, but this is the one I lined up for. Move it, pal, or you might find yourself getting a fist in *your* kisser."

Steve slapped his money on the counter and grabbed Lissa, bending her over his arm and kissing the living daylights out of her. When he lifted his head and stood her upright, she was the one ready to stagger. She was extremely careful not to, but shoved his money in the drawer and turned to the impatient next-in-line. Out of the corner of her eye, she saw Steve stalk back to his booth where his lineup was twenty deep again.

The afternoon wore on, and the money piled up. Lissa's lips ached, though not as much as her heart. She saw Rosa wander by, looking as disconsolate as she felt, and trying as hard not to show it.

"Caroline," she said, "I'm out of here now."

"Sure, okay. Thanks for your help. We made a good haul between the two of us."

"Rosa." Lissa caught up with her and took Rosa's hand. "Come and sit with me for a minute. I have a proposal for you."

"Yeah? What?"

"Something," Lissa said, "that I hope will bring a smile to your face. At least for a little while."

Rosa gave her a long, hard look. "I've been smiling," she said.

"Yes, but this time, I think you're going to mean it."

STEVE SAW LISSA coming toward his booth ten minutes before he was supposed to shut down at five, and didn't quite believe it. His line of hopeful Cinderellas had dwindled steadily until only a couple remained. They'd both already bought tickets before and tried on shoes. One of them had found a fit, and her name was put into the draw. They'd both received their kisses, and were now just chatting with him.

Lissa walked toward him accompanied by a bagpiper and a drummer, the skirl of the pipes and the thunder of the drum drawing eyes and bodies from all over the park. Lissa marched slowly, as if giving the crowd a chance to muster. That they did, until more people than Steve had even realized were there formed a vast crowd around his booth and up the slope across from it.

What the hell was she up to?

Whatever it was, he'd go along with it.

"My princess," he said, doffing his crown and bowing ceremoniously before her, as he had with every woman who visited his booth. "Have you come to try on your shoe?"

"Yes," she said, her voice icy, her eyes burning into his with utter disdain. So she hadn't come to beg his forgiveness, that was obvious. She hadn't come to apologize for mistrusting him. He considered telling her to get lost, but no, this was Lissa, and if her presence here meant there was the slightest chance he could fix whatever was wrong, he'd take it.

He slapped his crown back on his head and seated

her graciously on the throne. The bagpipe droned into silence, but the drummer kept up a steady, soft beat. "You really get into the spirit of things, don't you, sweet-cheeks?" Steve asked.

"You have no idea," she said. She placed her money on the counter. "It's nearly five. I've come to take my chance."

He wanted to tell her she had that without trying on a shoe, but the coldness in her eyes kept him silent. She tossed the line over the counter and a moment later, after the pole dipped sharply at its business end, she pulled it up. Of course, it didn't fit. Nor did the second one, but he knew, he *knew* the third one would. Every third shoe today had been the Birkenstock.

She stood. "I guess this just isn't my lucky day, Princie."

"No, wait," he said, "Each ticket buys three chances. Come, be seated, please, my lady." Steve cupped Lissa's shoulders in his hands. "Take one more chance on me," he whispered for her ears alone. "Lissa, please."

"No," Lissa said, not much to his surprise. She jerked free.

Quickly, before Steve could warn the kid behind the counter, Lissa handed the pole to Rosa and flipped the string over. "This third chance belongs to my faithful lady-in-waiting," she said loudly, clearly playing to the crowd. The rod tip dipped to signal the catch was on. Rosa pulled out her shoe.

Steve did not care for the triumphant smile Lissa directed at him as she shoved Rosa down onto the throne. "There, Prince Charming," she said, gesturing to the Birkenstock. "Try that one on for size."

Even before he knelt and put it on Rosa's foot, he

knew it would be a perfect fit. She pulled its mate from her capacious handbag and slipped it on too.

"So you see? A princess is as hard to spot in a crowd as a prince," Lissa said.

She signaled, and the strangest contraption Steve had ever seen came rolling toward his booth. It appeared to be made from the frame of a small car, with half of one of the huge orange metal balls used to float fish-farm equipment welded on top of it. It was pulled by four men in gray suits, men with long, skinny tails, and pointed rodentlike masks.

Before he could move or speak, Lissa said, "Well, Prince Charming, aren't you going to take your one, true princess to the stage and announce you've found her?" Like a coachman, she swung open the door of the carriage, swept into a bow and stood back. "Princess Rosa?" Rosa, with a smile as evil as a wicked witch in a fairy tale, stepped in, settled herself on the seat, then reached out her hand to Steve.

"My prince," she intoned in a witchy voice, "Come to me."

Steve felt a foot push hard against his royal-purple rump and tumbled into the vehicle, half falling across Rosa's lap. The crowd laughed and shouted and applauded, and the four "mice" towed the coach away toward the stage.

As they headed up the hill toward the bandstand, he glanced over his shoulder and saw the woman whose dragons he wanted to slay. She was pushing his coach up the slope. He groaned, and put a hand over his eyes. "Where the hell did I go wrong?" he muttered.

"The same place most men go wrong," Rosa said. "By lying to your woman, cheating on her and hurting her so bad you make her hate your guts."

He stared at her, rendered speechless by her outburst. He could see she meant every word, but it was too late to say anything, to explain. They'd arrived.

After Steve, Rosa and Lissa had mounted the bandstand, a local politician drew the names of the prizewinners, including those from the Cinderella booth—all but the last one. Lissa deftly took possession of the microphone.

"Now," she said, "the announcement we have all been waiting for. Prince Charming has found his one true princess, the lady who fits the shoe he has offered to every woman who took a chance at his booth. Prince Charming, would you like to present your princess to your subjects—and hers?"

Steve stared at her, then he stared at the grinning Rosa. How the hell had it ever come to this?

"Thank you, Ms. Wilkins," he said, and adjusted the mike to his height. "Ladies and gentlemen, loyal subjects all, may I present to you my princess, Rosa, um, Rosa—" He didn't know her last name! "Uh, the Lady Rosa of Madrona Cove."

He took Rosa's hand, drew her forward, then bent and kissed her fingertips.

"And," Lissa said, taking control of the mike again, "in accordance with Prince Charming's edict, the grandprize winner, Lady Rosa of Madrona Cove, is now about to select the escort of her choice for a fun and passion-filled two-week vacation at Happy Valley Hot Springs Resort."

She stepped back. "Lady Rosa?"

Rosa looked out at the crowd as if trying to find a likely candidate. She took her time, and the drummer, clearly sensing a need to heighten the tension, took up a soft, steady beat again. Rosa ambled to the edge of the stage, hands on her skinny hips, scanning the faces before her.

Steve was about to suggest she for Pete's sake get it over with when she whirled, pointed her finger at him and said, "I choose you, sweetie-pie. You look pretty darn good in purple tights. Fun and passion, huh? I haven't had much fun and passion in a long, long time and you look like a guy who could deliver." She reached up and patted his cheek, then slowly ran the tip of her finger down his chest toward the waist of his pants.

Steve truly thought he was going to faint before her finger finally came to a discreet halt. Sounds rose and faded in his ears. Black spots floated in front of his eyes. Then someone crowded past him and elbowed him out of the way as a voice boomed, "Like hell you pick him, woman! You want fun and passion and a two-week vacation, you take me."

"You go to hell, Frank Wilkins!" Rosa shouted. "I wouldn't take you to a dogfight, you fickle, two-timin' old goat. I know what you been up to, snugglin' up to that woman just 'cause she and her boy are gonna buy the inn. You think she's gonna be happy livin' in an attic with a bunch of old furniture you should have sent to the dump fifty years ago? You think she's gonna be good for this town? You think the Madrona Inn will still be standin' two years from now? You think *you* will?"

"You're damn right I will, and with you right beside me, woman! Nobody's getting that inn but me. And you. If you'll have me. And it."

"Oh...Frank..."

"Oh...Dad..."

Steve heard Lissa groan, saw her face crumple, but

couldn't reach out to her. Her father and Rosa, locked in an embrace that looked as if it might require a bucket of water to break, were in the way, along with the politician and the drummer. So was Pete, who for some reason had a smug grin on his face.

After a couple of minutes, Rosa pushed him away, her cheeks bright pink, her eyes sparkling. "Cut it out, you silly old coot," she said, the microphone on the bandstand catching her words and booming them out over the delighted crowd.

"Yeah. I guess you're right. I better save all my piss and vinegar for those two weeks of fun and passion we got coming to us. When we get back, we're going to be too busy running the inn to be doing a lot of canoodling."

"Dad! Listen to me." Lissa clung to her father's arm, the agony in her face like a knife in Steve's gut. "Oh, Dad, I should have told you. We didn't make it. It's after 5:30 and our bid's run out. Someone else bought the inn."

"Oh, no they didn't," he said. "*We* bought it."

Pete wheezed out a laugh. "That's what you think, old man." He pulled a piece of paper from his shirt pocket and waved it toward the crowd. "Where's John Drysdale? I got my check right here, and before each and every one of you, I'm going to put it in his hand. The inn is mine."

"The hell it is," Frank said. "Our bid was accepted at three o'clock this afternoon."

Pete's sweating face turned livid. "That's a lie! It's mine. I've—"

"Pete, Pete!" John Drysdale came rushing and pushing through the crowd and clambered onto the bandstand. He grabbed the manager's arm. "I told you not to count your chickens before 5:30. They came up with the money. I've been looking for you to tell you. Why the hell doesn't anybody in Madrona Cove answer their damn phone? Madrona Madness is exactly what this weekend is. But the inn is theirs. That's the law.''

"But...it can't be. I sacrificed. Sacrificed my principles, lowered my standards, did everything in my power to run the place at a loss so I could get it cheap and—''

"Pete, I think you'd better shut up," Drysdale said, dragging him to the ramp at the back of the stand and hustling him down it. It was too late, though. He'd said too much and everyone had heard him. Steve could almost feel sorry for the man.

Lissa continued to stare at her father. "But...where did the money come from?" she gasped.

"From that moldy old junk you and Rosa so despise," he said, flinging an arm around her shoulders, keeping his other firmly holding Rosa close to his side. "Loretta, Steve's mother, bought every last stick of it, except for the sleigh bed I, and my father before me, was born in. And for a pretty penny, too, more than enough to buy the inn. I advanced the proceeds of my sale to the committee's bank account. Our check's been accepted. I guess I've sold your heritage, Melissa, but since it's one you've never wanted, I figure you won't mind too much.''

He looked out over the crowd. "What I'm hoping is the committee will let me buy the inn. I know everyone was working to buy it out of sentiment and kindness toward me and my family, and I appreciate that, but there are other things this community needs just as badly, if not more. I'm stepping down as chairman as of today. I'll have a business to run and an inn to renovate.''

He looked down at Rosa, "And a bride to entertain.''

He paused, glanced from Lissa to Steve and added, "And maybe, soon, some grandkids who will want to become innkeepers and *will* accept it as their heritage.''

Still holding Rosa, he let Lissa go, and stepped down from the stage.

Lissa stood looking out at the still expectant crowd. Slowly, she reached out and shut off the mike. There was nothing more to say. There was nothing more to do. Nothing except…go home.

"My lady?'' Steve said softly, close to her ear.

"I'm not.''

"You are, you know. Come with me. Let me prove it.'' Before she could respond, he swept her up and carried her down the steps and straight to the carriage.

He lifted her in, climbed in behind her and drew her into his arms.

"I'm waiting,'' he said, his hand clasped around her braid.

Lissa looked at him for a long time. It took her a while to find the words. When she did, she nodded. "I'm sorry I misjudged you.''

"Uh-huh. I'm still waiting.''

"I'm sorry I didn't trust you enough to know you wouldn't have gone behind my back after having said you weren't here to buy the inn.''

"Yup.'' He looked at her as the carriage joggled into motion. "Still waiting.''

Lissa drew in a deep breath and held it for a moment before releasing it in a rush. "I love you,'' she said, and pulled his head down to hers.

He winced as the carriage hitched along, rocking un-
evenly, bumping their mouths together. "Good," he
said. "Then do me a favor?"

"If I can."

"Don't kiss me," he groaned. "For at least a
week."

"That long?" she complained as the carriage came
to a halt.

"At least."

"Sorry, you two, but we can't climb this hill," said
one of the mice—Reggie, if Lissa heard his voice right
through his muffling mask. "I guess you and your
prince walk from here, Liss."

"Not a chance," she said. "My prince is much too
pretty to walk. He might gets his silks and satins all
dusty."

She hopped out the left door of the carriage. "How
about I push again, and you guys pull?"

"You got it," Reggie said, and Lissa glanced in at
Steve, who was shaking with laughter.

"My princess," he said, jumping out and joining her
at the back of the carriage, leaning his weight into it.
"Will you ever let me slay a dragon for you?"

"Not likely," she said, puffing as the carriage made
its slow way to the top of the hill and out of the park.
"But maybe we can knock off a few together."

ANCHORED NEAR the shore in Gowland Harbor, not far
from home, but far enough away that she felt a world
apart from everyone she knew, Lissa lay curled against
Steve's warmth on a mattress on deck. Beneath them,
the boat rocked gently. Above them, the stars wheeled
lazily.

His hand moved lazily over her bottom, lingered on

her tattoo. "You know, I'd figured that when I finally saw it up close, I'd find a butterfly. I should have known. Who but my Lissa would have a hornet tattooed on her rear?"

"It'll only sting you if you don't behave," she said.

"Like this?"

She squirmed in pleasure. "It's a start."

But that, it seemed, was all it was. Steve wanted to talk. "Your dad said something," he murmured.

"My dad said lots of things." She raised herself on an elbow and looked down at him. "But you didn't. Why didn't you tell me right away Loretta was your mother? Why didn't you tell me why she came here?"

"It's what Frank wanted. He knew he had to free you from what you saw as an albatross, but until he was sure he could do it, he didn't want to get your hopes up."

"He knew that no matter how I griped and complained, I'd never leave him, or the inn, in the lurch."

"Exactly, and he wants you to have whatever kind of life you choose. But that thing he said, about grandkids..." He traced her eyebrows with one finger. "What do you think about that, Lissa?"

She grinned. "I wouldn't mind having a couple of grandchildren someday."

He laughed and pulled her down across his chest. "But you know what you have to do first, don't you?"

"No." She managed to sound mystified. "What?"

He told her and she sat up, pretending shock. "You mean it? *That's* where grandkids come from?"

"'Fraid so. So, what about it? That is, if you'll accept an unemployed diver as their father."

"I've been thinking about your unemployed state," she said. "How would you feel about becoming a partner in a marine-cruise business?'' She grinned. "I drive, you dive." He'd only sulked for a few minutes when she refused to let him run her boat.

"I'm sure we can work something out. But I'd rather talk about those grandkids and what we have to do first in order to get them."

"Well, if it's the only way," she said. "I guess I don't have much choice."

"I'm so glad you said that," he told her. "Because we've already taken one chance, and I wasn't sure you'd want to take another one."

"I'd take all kinds of chances with you."

"Good. Because we've used up everything in that box your friend gave you, and since I didn't know we'd be leaving port, I didn't do anything about it."

"Umm," she said a few minutes later. "When do you plan to do something?"

"About what?"

"About me. About my needs, which are growing needier and needier by the moment, sailor."

He took her hand and slid it down between them. "No more than mine, princess." He kissed her long and hard and deeply.

"Hey, look after those lips."

"I think they've healed," he said. "Love me, Lissa. Now."

"Now," she agreed. "And forever."

Take 4 bestselling love stories FREE

Plus get a FREE surprise gift!

DEBBIE MACOMBER

invites you to the

HEART OF TEXAS

Join Debbie Macomber as she brings you the lives
and loves of the folks in the ranching community
of Promise, Texas.

If you loved Midnight Sons—don't miss
Heart of Texas! A brand-new six-book series
from Debbie Macomber.

Available in February 1998
at your favorite retail store.

Heart of Texas by Debbie Macomber

Lonesome Cowboy	February '98
Texas Two-Step	March '98
Caroline's Child	April '98
Dr. Texas	May '98
Nell's Cowboy	June '98
Lone Star Baby	July '98

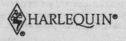

HARLEQUIN®

HPHRT1

Look for these titles—
available at your favorite retail outlet!

January 1998
Renegade Son by Lisa Jackson
Danielle Summers had problems: a rebellious child
and unscrupulous enemies. In addition, her Montana
ranch was slowly being sabotaged. And then there was
Chase McEnroe—who admired her land and desired her
body. But Danielle feared he would invade more than just
her property—he'd trespass on her heart.

February 1998
The Heart's Yearning by Ginna Gray
Fourteen years ago Laura gave her baby up for adoption,
and not one day had passed that she didn't think about
him and agonize over her choice—so she finally followed
her heart to Texas to see her child. But the plan to watch
her son from afar doesn't quite happen that way, once the
boy's sexy—*single*—father takes a decided interest in *her*.

March 1998
First Things Last by Dixie Browning
One look into Chandler Harrington's dark eyes and
Belinda Massey could refuse the Virginia millionaire nothing.
So how could the no-nonsense nanny believe the rumors that
he had kidnapped his nephew—an adorable, healthy little boy
who crawled as easily into her heart as he did into her lap?

BORN IN THE USA: Love, marriage—
and the pursuit of family!

Don't miss these Harlequin favorites by some of our top-selling authors!

HT#25733	THE GETAWAY BRIDE	$3.50 U.S. ☐	
	by Gina Wilkins	$3.99 CAN. ☐	
HP#11849	A KISS TO REMEMBER	$3.50 U.S. ☐	
	by Miranda Lee	$3.99 CAN. ☐	
HR#03431	BRINGING UP BABIES	$3.25 U.S. ☐	
	by Emma Goldrick	$3.75 CAN. ☐	
HS#70723	SIDE EFFECTS	$3.99 U.S. ☐	
	by Bobby Hutchinson	$4.50 CAN. ☐	
HI#22377	CISCO'S WOMAN	$3.75 U.S. ☐	
	by Aimée Thurlo	$4.25 CAN. ☐	
HAR#16666	ELISE & THE HOTSHOT LAWYER	$3.75 U.S. ☐	
	by Emily Dalton	$4.25 CAN. ☐	
HH#28949	RAVEN'S VOW	$4.99 U.S. ☐	
	by Gayle Wilson	$5.99 CAN. ☐	

(limited quantities available on certain titles)

AMOUNT	$ _____
POSTAGE & HANDLING	$ _____
($1.00 for one book, 50¢ for each additional)	
APPLICABLE TAXES*	$ _____
TOTAL PAYABLE	$ _____

(check or money order—please do not send cash)

To order, complete this form and send it, along with a check or money order for the total above, payable to Harlequin Books, to: **In the U.S.:** 3010 Walden Avenue, P.O. Box 9047, Buffalo, NY 14269-9047; **In Canada:** P.O. Box 613, Fort Erie, Ontario, L2A 5X3.

Name: _____

Address: _____ City: _____

State/Prov.: _____ Zip/Postal Code: _____

Account Number (if applicable): _____

*New York residents remit applicable sales taxes.
 Canadian residents remit applicable GST and provincial taxes.

Look us up on-line at: http://www.romance.net

075-CSAS

HBLJM98

As Seen on TV!

Free Gift Offer

With a Free Gift proof-of-purchase
from any Harlequin® book, you can receive
a beautiful cubic zirconia pendant.

This stunning marquise-shaped stone is a genuine cubic
zirconia—accented by an 18" gold tone necklace.
(Approximate retail value $19.95)

Send for yours today...
compliments of ◆ HARLEQUIN®

To receive your free gift, a cubic zirconia pendant, send us one original proof-of-purchase, photocopies not accepted, from the back of any Harlequin Romance®, Harlequin Presents®, Harlequin Temptation®, Harlequin Superromance®, Harlequin Love & Laughter®, Harlequin Intrigue®, Harlequin American Romance®, or Harlequin Historicals® title available at your favorite retail outlet, together with the Free Gift Certificate, plus a check or money order for $1.65 U.S./$2.15 CAN. (do not send cash) to cover postage and handling, payable to Harlequin Free Gift Offer. We will send you the specified gift. Allow 6 to 8 weeks for delivery. Offer good until March 31, 1998, or while quantities last. Offer valid in the U.S. and Canada only.

Free Gift Certificate

Name: _____

Address: _____

City: _____ State/Province: _____ Zip/Postal Code: _____

Mail this certificate, one proof-of-purchase and a check or money order for postage and handling to: HARLEQUIN FREE GIFT OFFER 1998. In the U.S.: 3010 Walden Avenue, P.O. Box 9071, Buffalo NY 14269-9057. In Canada: P.O. Box 604, Fort Erie, Ontario L2Z 5X3.

FREE GIFT OFFER   084-KEZ

ONE PROOF-OF-PURCHASE
To collect your fabulous FREE GIFT, a cubic zirconia pendant, you must include this original proof-of-purchase for each gift with the properly completed Free Gift Certificate.

084-KEZR2